Dmitri was so soundly asleep that he barely stirred when she slid out of his embrace.

Remembering the highs and lows of emotion he'd gone through in one evening, it was hardly surprising that he was exhausted, she thought as she hurried into her clothes.

Unable to bear the thought of leaving without some sort of farewell, she grabbed an empty envelope from the wastepaper basket beside his desk to pen a brief note.

Her heart was so full of all the things that she wanted to say that it was hard to know where to begin. In the end, all she could do was stick to the two most important points.

'I love you. I'll miss you,' she wrote, unhappy to discover that she'd already started crying when a tear splashed onto the words.

She didn't dare look back at him as she tried to prop the note somewhere he would find it as soon as he woke. Then there was no time to lose…

Dear Reader

Lauren, in my previous book, MORE THAN CARING, had grown self-sufficient because she had no family to rely on. In MORE THAN A GIFT, Laurel, by comparison, was being smothered by a family who seemed to criticise her every move. It was small wonder that she kept her thoughts and feelings to herself.

Sometimes it felt as if her much-loved nursing career was the only thing that kept her sane, and as for her growing relationship with Dmitri...

Then her own life took a turn and, with more than her own survival at stake, she had to leave Dmitri without ever telling him how much she cared.

Suddenly she she was on her own again, in a race against time, trying to decide which was more important. Her unknown twin or the man she loved.

I hope you enjoy unravelling her secrets.

Josie

MORE THAN A GIFT

BY
JOSIE METCALFE

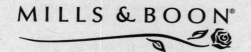

*First published in Great Britain 2002
Harlequin Mills & Boon Limited,
Eton House, 18-24 Paradise Road, Richmond, Surrey TW9 1SR*

© Josie Metcalfe 2002

ISBN 0 263 83107 8

*Set in Times Roman 10½ on 12¼ pt.
03-1202-46170*

*Printed and bound in Spain
by Litografía Rosés, S.A., Barcelona*

CHAPTER ONE

'I *DID* it,' Laurel breathed jubilantly, finally allowing her tense shoulders to slump with relief. 'I got away again.'

It felt as if she'd been driving for hours with her eyes glued to the rear-view mirror, her dread increasing with every big black car that appeared behind her.

Desperate to get as far away as possible, she'd pushed on until darkness had begun to fall and even then had barely dared to stop long enough to visit the Ladies' room. Perhaps it had been the failing light or the worsening weather or maybe her ploy of hiding her car among the enormous trucks that had put whoever was tailing her off the scent. She'd probably never know, but she was grateful for any piece of good luck that gave her the chance to get to the end of this journey.

After more than a year of searching she'd finally felt that she was on the right track, but she wouldn't really know until she reached Edenthwaite.

'Not that I know whether I'm even going in the right direction,' she muttered with a scowl, peering out through the windscreen at the worsening visibility.

The narrow road she was following suddenly twisted into another series of bends and she tightened her grip on the steering-wheel.

It would have been far easier and faster if she'd

been able to stay on the motorway for another half-hour or so, especially with the first spits of rain misting the windows, but she hadn't dared. To have come so close to the hospital where Lauren worked only to be stopped before she could meet her...well, it didn't bear thinking about. It would mean that everything she'd suffered through her miserable childhood had been a waste of time, especially now that she knew why her father...

'No! He's *not* my father!' she spat angrily, still incensed by the pretence she'd unwittingly been living all her life.

All those years of wondering why she was so unlovable that he'd barely spared her a word unless it had been to criticise and demean. All those years of trying so hard to turn herself into the daughter he wanted her to be, a daughter he would approve of.

Even now, a year after the revelation, she could hardly credit the simple series of events that had finally exposed the deception.

It had been sheer fluke that she'd seen the letter addressed to her before it had been taken through to his study with the rest of the mail. She had no doubt, now, that the contents would have been destroyed if *he* had seen them first. Then she would never have discovered that she'd been adopted, or that there was another—

'Damn!' she exclaimed, her rambling thoughts brought to an abrupt end as the back end of the car slewed without warning, the wheels spinning frantically for several seconds before they regained traction.

Careful to keep her foot well away from both brake

and accelerator, she allowed the car to slow naturally, her hands shaking as she tentatively straightened the wheels. Surely the temperature hadn't dropped enough, yet, for black ice to have started to form on the road.

She risked a quick glance at her watch and did some mental calculations, immeasurably relieved when she realised that she must be little more than five or so miles from Edenthwaite now.

Tentatively, she pressed on the accelerator again, reassured by the tyres' renewed grip on the road. She should arrive safely long before the weather became a real problem, even if it was dark by the time she reached her destination.

She'd only travelled another mile when the dark car swung around the bend in front of her, travelling far too fast for the road conditions. Almost in slow motion, Laurel saw the moment when the driver lost control, his headlights veering towards the unforgiving stone wall at the side of the road. The tyres squealed and she held her breath as he tried to steer the heavy vehicle out of the skid. For just a second she thought he'd been successful, only to realise that he was now heading straight towards her.

Reflexively, she twisted the wheel, her only thought to avoid the impending crash.

Suddenly everything was happening too fast for her to register each individual event. She had an impression of hands frantically turning the steering-wheel in the other car, eyes and mouth open in matching horror, her own car striking the limestone wall a glancing blow as the black car screeched its way along her paintwork.

Then the black car disappeared from her sight as her car began to spin. It seemed as if she was whirling around for ever, going faster and faster as she travelled down the slope of the hill. The headlights picked out a wildly spinning kaleidoscope of images right up till she broadsided the wall for a second time, then all she could see was the dark arc of the sky as the car toppled onto its side, crashing through the top of the wall and down into the field below.

'OhGod, OhGod, OhGod,' Laurel heard herself whimpering when everything finally stopped moving and she realised she was still alive.

It took her a moment to catch her breath and realise that she was virtually suspended from her seat belt, hanging almost completely upside down. Even so, something made her grab hold of the steering-wheel to drag herself close enough to switch off the engine.

It was awkward to reach, especially as she had to be careful not to cause any further damage with the restricting seat belt.

'Was that the right thing to do?' she whispered into the sudden silence, curving her hands protectively around herself. One half of her brain was telling her that it was the best way to minimise the risk of fire. She didn't yet know how long it was going to take to clamber out of her awkward position. Having survived the crash, she certainly didn't want to burn to death. There was more than her own life at stake here.

It wasn't until she realised how completely dark it was outside now that she wondered if she might have made a mistake.

Without the engine switched on, she couldn't have

any of the lights on, so no one would be able to see her.

'Especially with the car tucked behind the wall like this,' she muttered as she craned her neck to try to look around.

The car gave a metallic groan as it shifted in response to her movement and she froze, suddenly aware that while she knew there was a wall close to one side of the car she had absolutely no idea what lay the other side.

Long-ago geography lessons flashed into her mind and she actually remembered drawing diagrams to explain the way glaciation had shaped the scenery around Edenthwaite.

'Flat-bottomed, U-shaped valleys with steep sides,' she whispered, the illustrations clear in her head. She groaned when she remembered looking at the map that morning as she'd planned the fastest route north. She'd seen the switchback wriggles of the smaller side roads as they fought their way up out of one valley and over the rocky limestone tops before plunging in an equally dizzying drop into the next.

Depending which bit of road she was on when that car had headed straight for her, the scene outside her window could be a flat valley floor, a limestone pavement at a thousand or more feet up, or any point in between.

'Well, whatever's out there, I can't stay here all night,' she declared firmly. 'It would be one thing to stay with the car if I'd broken down at the side of the road, but if I just hang around in here, I might still be waiting for help when Christmas comes.' She gave a wry chuckle at her unintentional pun. 'Hanging around…like a bauble on a Christmas tree.'

She stretched out one hand to reach for the release mechanism for her belt, needing to relieve the pressure across her body. She was going to have some bruises but at least the belt had prevented her from sustaining a broken neck.

'And how about you?' she murmured softly, still cradling the swell of her belly with her other hand while she tried to work out how to release the seat belt. 'I bet you're glad you were cushioned by all that amniotic fluid.'

As if in answer, a tiny limb gave her hand a resounding thump.

Laurel smiled as she circled the spot with her fingertips. 'All right. It shouldn't be long before I get us out of here…although what difference it will make to you, I don't know. You seem to have spent the last few months turning somersaults, so hanging upside down is no novelty.'

Frustrated with her lack of success with the belt, she twisted to get her other hand close enough to help and the car shuddered again, this time almost feeling as if it had shifted a little way along the ground.

Laurel froze again with her heart in her mouth. For several endless seconds she held her breath, only releasing it when all stayed still and quiet.

Only it wasn't quite quiet. There was a strange new ticking sound, now that she concentrated. It wasn't the sound of the engine cooling down, or the regular metallic sort of sound that a clock would make. It was far softer and more random against the window beside her.

It took her several moments to track the source down, and the answer sent a shiver down her spine.

'It's started snowing!' she whimpered.

She'd thought it too dark outside to see anything but as she stared in disbelief at the swirling flickers of brightness that had begun to land on the window beside her head, she knew she'd been wrong.

So far, most of it seemed to be whirling around in the air. There was little more than a sprinkle settling on the ground or over the vehicle, but that could change all too quickly.

'Please…no! Don't do this to me!' she moaned.

Her situation had been bad enough before. If it carried on snowing, it would become impossible.

She shivered as she forced herself to take an inventory.

'For a start, it's getting colder,' she stated aloud, knowing that it wasn't just because she didn't dare risk running the car heater. 'And if it keeps snowing, not only will it cover the car, but it'll cover up any signs of where I went off the road, so no one will know where to look.'

Another sound interrupted her, so unexpected that it took her several seconds to realise what it was.

'A car!' she shrieked when her brain finally put all the clues together. 'There's a car coming!'

She wriggled forward, trying to reach far enough to sound the horn. It was easier to see what she was aiming for now, as the approaching headlights reflected off the walls on either side of the road to spill into the topsy-turvy compartment.

A sudden flash of light swept across her as the headlights poured through the gateway further along the wall and caught her mirror just as she found the horn.

The sight of the dark silhouette behind the lights was just ominous enough to make her hesitate and the opportunity was lost.

'You *stupid* woman,' she railed as the vehicle swept on by without a pause. 'So what if it was *them*? At least you'd have some hope of getting out of here alive.'

For a moment she felt utterly helpless and had to fight the threat of tears. Was this what it had all come to? That unhappy childhood and the steadily increasing desperation of her teenage years when she'd actually begun to believe that her mind was unbalanced. Then the revelations in that letter and her determination to find out if they were true.

She'd come so close. In fact, she was almost certain that Lauren Scott was the one person who would be willing to fill in the missing pieces of the puzzle. Lauren, who lived about five miles away from this very spot and might as well have been five thousand for all the good it did.

A swift kick just under her ribs broke into her dismal train of thoughts with a jolt, and a second one was enough to stiffen her resolve.

'You're right,' she muttered with new determination. 'I've come this far and I'm not giving up now. After all, I've got you to think about.'

She snatched a shallow breath, anything deeper being impossible while hanging in this position, and twisted towards the seat-belt release, resolved not to let it beat her this time.

She'd completely forgotten about the way the car

rocked when she moved too quickly, and this time freezing in position when the metal panels groaned wasn't enough. With a lurch and a shudder she felt the vehicle shift towards the unknown blackness outside, the momentum growing as it began to roll.

'No!' she screamed, helplessly trying to brace herself against the movement, even though she knew she was powerless to prevent it happening.

With the unearthly groaning and crashing going on all around her, the car rolled from its side to its roof and almost onto the other side while Laurel was tossed as helplessly as a puppet on a string.

She was utterly convinced that the next revolution would take her over the edge of an escarpment to her death in the valley far below, but then her head swung into the frame of the door beside her and everything went black.

Dmitri glared out at the snow swirling across the road in front of him and swore out loud.

'That's all I needed,' he groaned, deliberately reverting to English. He tried reminding himself that there would be a great deal more snow than this in his native country, but it didn't help his temper.

'If only I'd done something about it as soon as I saw her car,' he muttered. 'Now, who knows *which* road she's taken. It could be months before I get that close again.'

Hearing the words aloud made him pause.

Months?

Was he really willing to put his life on hold while he searched the length and breadth of the country to track the wretched woman down again? It had taken him two weeks just to track down which hospital she'd been working at last, and it had taken all the charm he'd been able to muster to persuade one of her neighbours to remember that she'd mentioned a possible Christmas break in Cumbria.

He couldn't imagine the magnitude of the coincidence that had put the two of them on the same motorway at exactly the same time...and then he'd lost her again.

So, he had a decision to make. He had another two weeks before he had to make a decision about the date of his return to work in Russia, two weeks that he could spend visiting Babushka Ana and getting his life in order, or he could spend it trying to complete his search for Laurel.

He'd come so close this afternoon that he could almost have reached out and touched her car. If he hadn't decided to bide his time...

But did he really want to spend two precious weeks chasing down a woman who'd left him without a backward glance? Shouldn't he go back to Babushka Ana as soon as possible? She'd been so frail last time he'd seen her. Who knew how long she had left?

Not that she knew who he was half the time, but still...she had been the one constant in his life for so many years that he couldn't help the guilt when he thought of her days passing endlessly without family to visit her.

But if a few more days or weeks meant finding out what had happened to Laurel, why she'd disappeared like that...

As ever, her image was clear in his mind—the long, softly curling hair that made him think of

Christmas angels, the sweetly expressive face and those fascinating amber eyes. It had been the hidden shadows in those eyes that had first caught his attention a year ago when he'd joined the staff at the hospital where she'd just been finishing her training.

Not that she'd done anything to attract his attention. Far from it.

In fact, it had taken him several weeks of concerted effort before he'd realised that, far from downplaying her beauty, she'd actually been totally oblivious to it.

He still marvelled at her innocence, and the unexpectedly passionate way she'd responded to him, even as he railed at the way she'd suddenly disappeared from the hospital and his life, apparently uncaring of the fact that they had an ongoing relationship.

It was that relationship and, yes, he wasn't too proud to admit it, a measure of injured ego that had prompted him to spend this time trying to find out why she'd left.

But was he willing to spend more weeks tracking Laurel down? The heat that poured through him when he remembered the way she'd responded to his kisses gave him his answer. Yes, he was, even if he gained no more than the satisfaction of finding out why she'd run away.

The heat became the slow burn of anger and determination that had prompted him to plan his final quest during the last days of his job in England, and had accompanied him throughout his search. Then the car wheels gave a sudden slew sideways and he had to drag his concentration back to the road. He wouldn't be in a fit state to search for anyone if he were trapped in a heap of crumpled metal at the side of the road.

'How much further is it to this place?' he muttered, not even daring to glance at the map he'd left open on the passenger seat beside him. 'What was it called? Something that made me think of the Garden of Eden.'

He pulled a face at the dimly perceived scenery through which he was passing. It had looked quite spectacular until the light had faded and the snow had started falling. Now it looked far from idyllic, just somewhere on the road to...Edenthwaite! That was it! Although why Laurel wanted to go there was way beyond him.

He'd been so sure that she'd been enjoying her work as a newly qualified nurse, and enjoying the relationship they'd been forging together. Obviously, he'd been wrong or she wouldn't have left like that, without even a word to...

'What was that?' He took his foot off the pedal and peered towards the ragged top of the stone wall beside him and the metallic flash that had caught his eye.

As it receded in his rear-view mirror he realised that someone must have crashed into it at some time because the flash had been a reflection from broken shards of glass or a mirror.

'Thank goodness it didn't happen tonight,' he murmured when he noted the lack of tyre tracks in the layer of snow beginning to gather across the road and on the limestone blocks that made up the bordering walls. 'I pity anyone who crashes up here tonight. If the snow keeps falling like this, it could be days before anyone finds them.'

With new caution in each movement, he allowed the car to pick up a bit of speed again. There was no point loitering in the middle of nowhere in this weather when he could be booking into the hotel in Edenthwaite.

'I'll make some phone calls tonight to find out where she's staying. If she was making for Edenthwaite, it's probably because she's hoping to get a job in the hospital, or she's about to take up a post there. By tomorrow, I should be able to start asking some questions,' he said firmly. 'There must be some reason why she's been moving about so much—some reason why she was heading in this particular direction—and I'm going to find out what it is.'

Then, perhaps, he'd be able to go back to Russia with a clear conscience. At least he wouldn't be left with the nagging feeling that he should have tried just a little harder to find the woman who was never very far from his mind.

'Where are all the cars when I need them?' Laurel groaned, her eyes fixed on the cock-eyed view in the mirror. At least she wasn't totally upside down any more. The car seemed to be on its side.

The cold had seeped into the car slowly at first but there was no heat left at all now. She was shivering all the time, and her head was aching after the collision with the door frame. She had no idea how long she'd been unconscious but her brain was still functioning well enough to appreciate the irony of the situation.

'After all this time of keeping a low profile and

making sure I don't do anything to draw attention to myself,' she groaned. How many times had she caught sight of her pursuer and known that it had been time to move on yet again? It must be four or five times since she'd read that letter and realised the significance of it.

Not that she *had* realised the full significance until she'd made a few enquiries. The whole thing had seemed utterly fantastic…totally unbelievable…until she'd taken a chance and had barged into the lawyer's office without the courtesy of an appointment and had demanded some straight answers.

'I'm a *twin*,' she whispered, feeling the smile spread over her chilly face again, the delight growing with each repetition. 'She's somewhere out there—in Edenthwaite, perhaps—and when I find her, I'll finally be able to get the answers to fill in all the rest of the pieces to the puzzle.'

And there were so many questions, more with every day that had passed since she'd read that fateful letter.

Her mother's letter.

Her *real* mother.

She had a copy of it with her now, sewn into the lining of her coat, but for safekeeping had lodged the original and the will and birth certificates that had accompanied it with her mother's solicitor until she completed her search.

She didn't need to see the faded script on the first page to recall the heartbroken words, apparently written just hours after she'd given birth and had had to watch her precious babies being taken away for others to nurture into adulthood.

The first time she'd read the letter, she'd been shocked, then overwhelmed with anger at the deception that had shaped her life. It had taken her several months before she'd been able to find sympathy in her heart for the mother who had abandoned her then deliberately distanced herself from any contact.

Laurel closed her eyes against the hot prick of tears, cradling her hands over the swell of her own child. It hadn't been until she'd realised that she was pregnant and had felt that instant flood of maternal love that she'd been able to understand how a mother would do anything to make sure her child was taken care of, even give her up for adoption.

She was just grateful that society had changed enough in the last twenty-eight years that she could make her own choices, not have them forced upon her by appalled family and friends.

And they *would* be appalled if they knew what she'd been doing for the last year.

She gave a brief wry chuckle when she realised just how close to twelve months it had been since she'd left the only home she'd known and had tried to disappear.

It would be Christmas in just a few days, and exactly one year ago she'd been a meekly dutiful part of the lavish planning and preparations for her wedding.

She still didn't know whether Grant had been privy to her father...no, *not* her father...to Robert Wainwright's machinations. When she'd realised what had been going on, she hadn't paused even long enough to leave him a note and hadn't dared to contact him in the meantime.

Not that she believed for a moment that she'd left Grant with a broken heart. As far as she could tell, theirs had been a marriage brokered solely in pursuit of financial gain.

One thing that had persuaded her into agreeing to it had been the fact that she would finally be escaping from Robert's incessant criticism. It would be such a relief not to have to pretend any more that she was still taking those wretched tablets and to be able to live her own life. The fact that she would finally be able to wholeheartedly follow the nursing profession she'd fought so hard for had been enough to convince her to accept Grant's proposal.

It wasn't as if she'd had any other suitors lining up, not with Robert keeping an eagle eye on every spare moment when she hadn't been on duty. Anyway, she'd never really wanted a man in her life. A lifetime under the overbearing control of one had made her wary about any sort of social interaction. It had been enough for her that she'd finally completed her training as a nurse.

Laurel sighed when she remembered just how long she'd had to campaign to be allowed to apply for a place and her surprise when her mother...no, not her mother, Robert's wife, had added her weight to the argument in her favour.

She would always see the day of her interview as a milestone in her life. For a few moments she'd wondered if she'd made an enormous mistake when she'd explained in detail how she'd become addicted to tranquillisers and the steps she'd taken to rid herself of the problem.

Looking back, she believed that it had been her

willingness to consider herself on probation and the offer to permit blood tests at any time to confirm that she was 'clean' that had prompted them to give her the chance she'd wanted.

Those years had been hard work but she didn't regret a single bedpan. Not only had they given her a way to escape the poisonous atmosphere that seemed to surround her whenever she was in the same room as Robert Wainwright, they'd also made her realise that she'd found the purpose to her life.

And that wasn't all. There was another, even more important reason.

If she hadn't fought to get out from under Robert Wainwright's thumb—if she hadn't insisted that she wanted to train as a nurse—she'd never have been in the right place at the right time to meet Dmitri.

This time the smile was bitter-sweet, muted by the pang of loss that surrounded her heart.

It hurt to know that never again would she see the man she loved. After the way she'd had to leave him, he probably wouldn't want to have anything to do with her, but that didn't mean that she regretted meeting him. Far from it.

Laurel didn't need to have him in front of her to be able to picture him perfectly, starting with those mesmerising eyes.

CHAPTER TWO

'Excuse me?'

Fear had been Laurel's first reaction at being accosted, and she'd frozen. It had always been her first emotion in those days. Fear that someone had finally seen behind her deception and tracked her down. She hadn't seen how they could have, since she'd changed the name she was known by on the ward, but still, with the necessity of at least one person in the admin department knowing her legal name so that she'd been able to be paid, there had always been a risk that something could get back to Robert Wainwright.

The softly spoken voice behind her had a definite accent but it wasn't one that Laurel recognised. Neither did she recognise the shiver of awareness that the velvety sound had on her nerves.

She forced herself to turn, and looked up into the most amazing eyes she'd ever seen.

They were grey, but not like any grey she'd ever seen before. They didn't look the cold colour of steel but almost as if they carried the searing heat of molten silver, and set against the intriguing slant of lean cheeks and surrounded by long dark lashes they seemed more mysterious than ever.

For several long seconds Laurel stared into them, almost mesmerised by their intensity. It wasn't until he blinked that those sinfully long lashes broke the spell and she realised that she hadn't said a word.

'I'm sorry. Can I help you?' At least she hadn't dropped the armful of clean sheets she was carrying.

'I hope so. Can you tell me, which way to *rye-byonak*?'

'Ryeby—what?' Laurel asked, wondering if her brain was so scrambled that she couldn't understand simple English any more.

'I'm sorry,' he said with a rueful grin. 'I was thinking of home—of Russia—and sometimes the wrong words come out. I should have said I was looking for the...the babies. Neonatal department.'

'I'm going that way myself. I can show you,' she offered, hoping her cheeks weren't as red as they felt. His eyes had hardly left her face since she'd turned round and she was now wondering if she'd got a coffee moustache, or something. She would have to check as soon as she had a moment. It was imperative that she didn't draw even the most innocent attention to herself, not until she'd accomplished what she'd set out to do.

'Here. Let me take those for you,' he offered, and before she even realised what he was going to do, let alone argue about the need, he'd scooped the heavy pile of linen out of her arms and tucked them easily under one arm.

And all she could think about was the fact that she could smell the scent of soap on his skin.

'You work in the department?' he asked as they set off, and she wondered if he was having to shorten his stride to allow her to keep up with him. She wasn't particularly short at five feet eight, but guessed that he must be at least six feet and probably an inch or two more.

And every inch of it seemed as lean and powerful as one of those swimmers she'd seen on television, practising for the next Olympics. He might be dressed in a smart charcoal-grey suit and white shirt at the moment, but she could just imagine what he'd look like in a pair of those skin-tight shorts, or…

Whoa! Enough!

What on earth was happening to her? She'd *never* been the sort to fantasise about men, let alone *naked* men. And all he'd done had been to carry a pile of sheets and ask her…

'Oh, yes!' she said hurriedly, suddenly realising that he was still waiting for an answer. 'I work on the neonatal ward—well, I've only recently started in the department. It's my first post since I qualified.'

'And was this an assignment, or was it something that you have chosen?'

His expression was so intent that she could almost imagine that her answer mattered more than if it was just for the sake of conversation.

'Oh, I chose it,' she said, feeling quite flustered. She just wasn't accustomed to being the focus of anyone's attention, unless they were looking to find fault. 'It's what I've always wanted to do.'

'I hope it meets your expectations,' he said with a thoughtful nod, then continued softly, so softly that, coloured by his exotic accent, she couldn't be sure she'd heard him correctly, 'You will be good for the babies.'

That had sounded like a compliment, something else that she wasn't accustomed to hearing and had no idea how to respond to. Thank goodness they had reached the ward.

'Sister should be in her office. Shall I show you where…?'

'No, thank you. That won't be necessary,' he said with a smile that almost had her swallowing her tongue. This man was more deadly than anything the old Soviet Union might have once had in its nuclear arsenal. 'I can find my way around the ward. I just have trouble finding my way around the hospital at the moment.'

He relinquished his hold on the pile of sheets.

'Perhaps you need to drop a trail of breadcrumbs so you can find your way back,' she suggested with a grin of her own, only realising how flippant she must have sounded when she reached the linen cupboard. That was hardly the right way to go about keeping a low profile.

'Get a grip on yourself,' she muttered under her breath as she stacked the shelves neatly. They couldn't afford to run low on clean linen when their patients were among the most fragile and susceptible to infection in the whole hospital.

At least disposable nappies had eliminated one set of supply problems. She could just imagine how many traditional cloth ones would have been used in a day.

Now she needed to let Sister know that she'd returned from her errand and find out about her next task. That was one thing about working in a busy unit like this, there was so much going on and so many things to do that she was learning something new every day. Still, it would be nice when she was proficient enough to do more than assist her more senior colleagues.

'Roll on the day when I'm not one of the lowest of the low,' she murmured. Having had to fight to be allowed to do her nursing training, she was several years older than most newly qualified staff, and she was human enough to feel a twinge of resentment when she was being ordered to do relatively menial tasks by much younger women. 'And as there's no way I'll be moving up the ladder until they're sure that I'm competent enough, that situation can only be remedied by time and hard work.'

She consciously straightened her shoulders and lifted her chin. The fact that her flight from home had also cost her the plum post she'd been offered at the hospital where she'd done her training was just another thing to lay at her family's feet. At least her 'record' as a former tranquilliser addict was in the past, buried by the hospital at which she'd done her training. They'd actually told her that after watching her closely over the last three years, they had no fear that it would ever interfere with her work.

'Ah, there she is, Sister Richards! My rescuer!' exclaimed a newly familiar voice, and Laurel's breath caught in her throat.

'Thank you for rescuing him for me, Laurel. I wouldn't want to lose him,' her superior said, but although she was speaking to Laurel, her eyes never left the lean man at her side.

Laurel could all too easily understand why, especially if he was in the habit of smiling like that. What she didn't know was whether there was something of a personal nature between the two of them, neither did she know why just the thought of it made her feel strangely hollow inside.

'We didn't introduce ourselves properly,' he said, completely ignoring Melanie Richards's possessive-sounding words as he held a hand out towards Laurel.

'Oh, she's Laurel Wright, one of our most junior staff,' her superior said dismissively, her eyes still fixed on the man like a starving woman gazing at a giant box of Belgian chocolates. 'This is Dr Ros— Rostro—'

'Rostropovich,' he supplied, tightening his hand fractionally around Laurel's when she would have withdrawn it immediately. 'Dmitri Rostropovich. It would probably be easier if you called me—'

'Pleased to meet you, Dr Rostropovich,' Laurel said without any difficulty, and had to fight a smile at her superior's visible chagrin. Stumbling over pronouncing his name was all the evidence Laurel had needed that they were not as close as the younger woman wanted them to be. 'Do you spell that the same way as the famous cellist?'

Having retrieved her hand, she wrapped the other one around it, surprised that she couldn't feel the flash of heat that had been generated when his hand had touched hers. She was going to have to revise her scepticism over those scenes in romance novels where there was an electric connection between the hero and heroine the first time they touched.

Not that she was anybody's heroine, least of all his.

'It's spelt exactly the same, although I don't think there's any family connection. Do you like his music?'

'Some of it, especially his recording of—'

'Laurel doesn't really have time to stand chatting about music,' Melanie Richards pointed out with a disgruntled scowl. 'It's time for Staff Nurse Norris to go for her break, isn't it, Nurse? You're supposed to be taking over monitoring baby Sweeny, aren't you?'

It was news to Laurel but she wasn't about to turn down the chance to do some hands-on nursing for a change. Up till this moment Sister Richards had seemed to be deliberately keeping her to menial tasks.

'Perhaps we will be able to talk of music another time,' Dmitri said politely as Laurel turned to cross the ward towards her charge. 'In the meantime, if you will permit, I will come with you to have a look at this baby Sweeny who needs monitoring.'

Laurel caught a glimpse of the hastily hidden flash of anger in her superior's eyes and blinked in surprise.

Surely the woman realised that it had been a purely professional decision for the good-looking doctor to accompany her? Melanie was a beautiful young woman with the sort of curves that Laurel could only sigh for. After all those years of 'blunt speaking' by Robert Wainwright, she knew only too well that she had few charms to attract a man's eye. Least of all now, when she was being so careful not to draw attention to herself. If Robert Wainwright tracked her down before she found her sister, her rebellion would all have been in vain. She had no doubt that the man would be desperate enough by now to resort to all sorts of underhand tactics to achieve his aim.

Her heart gave a thud of fear before she deliberately set her thoughts on a different track...such as the handsome doctor's completely unexpected response towards her.

Had her attempts at merging into the background completely failed today? Dmitri Rostropovich's eyes seemed to be spending an inordinate amount of time looking in her direction. And the only reason she knew that was because, even though her hands were busy noting down the readings of Jason Sweeny's temperature, blood pressure and pulse from the electronic monitors onto his charts, her own gaze seemed magnetically attracted to him.

Unfortunately, Jason's mother, who had rarely left his bedside once she'd been released from her own, had noticed her preoccupation.

'He's a good looker, isn't he, Nurse?' she prompted slyly, and Laurel felt the flush of heat travelling inexorably upward from her throat to her tightly restrained hair. How could she have forgotten just how sharp-eyed some people could be when there wasn't much else to watch?

She bit her tongue as she hung the clipboard on the end of the high-tech trolley, hoping desperately to find some way of avoiding an answer.

'Well, Nurse?' he prompted, startling her into looking up into the wicked gleam in his eyes. He'd leaned himself against the column supporting the monitor displays while he'd chatted easily with Mrs Sweeny. Now he'd folded his arms across his chest as though he had the whole day to wait for her answer. 'Do you agree with Mrs Sweeny?'

The pair of them exchanged a telling glance, grey eyes meeting blue, each knowing that they had put her on the spot.

Laurel felt the familiar anxiety start to swamp her, the feeling that she just wanted the ground to open up and swallow her. And what was worse, she couldn't drag her eyes away from him.

If he could read her thoughts and feelings in her eyes, what would he think of her cowardly nature?

He wouldn't know about the years she'd spent as the butt of Robert Wainwright's caustic wit. Then, defiance had only earned her the label of 'disturbed child' and another handful of tranquillisers.

In the end, her only defence had been silence and stoicism while her resentment had grown, and in her undrugged moments her determination to find some way out of the destructive situation.

Then, for the first time in her life, she felt a sudden surge of something new. She didn't know what it was or what was causing it. Could it be something to do with the expression in a certain pair of liquid silver eyes?

'I suppose he's *quite* good-looking, Mrs Sweeny,' she admitted grudgingly. She flicked her gaze over him from head to foot and back again, his elegant grey suit doing more to enhance his lean physique than disguise it, then made sure there was more than a hint of doubt in her intonation. 'That's if you like them long and skinny.'

Mrs Sweeny burst out laughing.

'That told you, didn't it?' She laughed gleefully up at Dmitri Rostropovich, her perpetually worried eyes brightening briefly with a flash of humour. 'I'm so glad that we women are getting a chance to put a man in his place these days.'

Laurel found herself holding her breath, waiting for his response. What on earth had possessed her to talk to him like that? Apart from the foolishness of drawing attention to herself, she knew better than to provoke a man into anger by answering back.

Then he chuckled.

'Oh, yes, Mrs Sweeny. I certainly like a woman who knows how to put a man in his place,' he agreed. 'The only trouble is, most men don't know their place until a woman shows them.'

There was something in his gaze that made Laurel feel warm inside, almost as if she were basking in the warmth of a summer's day, and it was a feeling she wanted to explore. Perhaps…

'Haven't you finished that yet, Nurse?' Melanie Richards's voice snapped, dispelling the warmth with a blast of frigid disapproval. 'I thought you were supposed to be fully qualified for this job, but you're as slow as the greenest student.'

'I'm sorry—' Laurel began, automatically apologising even though she knew she hadn't done anything wrong.

'That would be my fault,' Dmitri interrupted smoothly, straightening up from his relaxed slouch against the column supporting the monitoring equipment to his full six feet plus. Laurel couldn't help noticing that there was no smile in evidence any more either. 'My interruptions might have delayed her but they didn't interfere with the standard of Laurel's work.'

'Oh, well, I…' Melanie began backtracking, fast.

'And she's got very gentle hands, too,' Mrs Sweeny butted in. 'Not like some of the nurses. Sometimes you get the feeling that they're trying to do too many jobs at once and doing none of them well.'

'Yes, well, Staff Nurse Norris is back now, so you can take these papers to Administration,' Melanie ordered repressively, before turning her attention on the handsome doctor with a renewed smile. 'Have you got time for a cup of tea, or perhaps you'd prefer coffee?'

'Actually, I know I'm not due on duty until tomorrow, but I think I'd prefer to take a trip around the department, if that's all right with you.'

'Of course it is. And I can answer any questions as we go round,' Laurel heard her gush, and gritted her teeth as she shouldered her way through the door and paused to hear the security latch click firmly closed behind her. Did the woman have no idea about subtlety?

'That would take up far too much of your valuable time,' she heard him say firmly. 'I would rather familiarise myself with the department in my own way, if you don't mind. If I have any questions, I can ask you later, perhaps?'

'Well, of course. If that's the way you would prefer it.'

Melanie's annoyance at having her invitation turned down was so clear that Laurel couldn't help laughing to herself as she set off on her time-wasting errand. It was good to know that their new doctor wasn't going to be taken in by a woman with a pretty face. He definitely knew his own mind.

Perhaps he would even be able to do something about making better use of her presence in the unit. Each of their little charges needed the equivalent of five and a half nurses and they were desperately short of fully qualified staff. Even though she lacked experience, it just didn't make sense to send her off on errands that could just as easily have been done by a porter.

The smile put on Laurel's face by Dmitri's rebuff of Melanie Richards's cloying attention didn't last for long. How could it when inside her head there was a maelstrom of thoughts whirling and colliding in chaotic confusion?

And all because of Dr Dmitri Rostropovich.

What was it about the man?

She'd only met him this morning and already it looked as if he'd caused mayhem in the calm, ordered life she'd created for herself.

For a start, he seemed to have completely scrambled her emotions. Not so very long ago she'd been in the middle of preparations for a wedding to a man who'd never even made her heart skip a beat in all the time she'd known him. Now she'd met a man who created wild Latin-American dance rhythms in her blood with nothing more than the sound of his voice or a wicked smile.

One part of her—a very large part—was only too willing to explore these enticing new sensations. The other part was far more sane and rational, reminding her of the reasons why she was here in the hospital at all.

If she'd stayed where she had been she'd be a married woman by now, browbeaten into obedience by Robert Wainwright purely because she'd realised it had been her only escape from a life lived permanently under his thumb.

The sole reason why she'd been at the right place and time to meet Dmitri was because she was searching for her sister, and the only way she'd been able to do that was by changing her name and moving away from everything and everyone she knew.

Still, the feminine side of her couldn't resist the suggestion that Dmitri found her attractive. Well, he seemed to prefer her company to Melanie's, at least.

Who knew what might develop over the next days and weeks? For the first time in a very long time she was actually looking forward to finding out.

'If I'd known then what I know now,' she muttered through chattering teeth, her breath emerging in a ghostly cloud, visible even in the dark of the car.

She had no idea how long she'd been here. At this time of the year any time between four o'clock and seven o'clock would be dark whichever end of the day they appeared.

With a feeling of dread she realised that it must still be evening, and the only reason it seemed lighter was because the snow was beginning to accumulate around the car.

She almost regretted her return to the stark reality of her present situation. It was far more pleasant re-living those first heady days after she'd met Dmitri.

She glanced at the luminous dial on her watch and was surprised to see that it was only just past four in the afternoon.

Unfortunately, she didn't know whether any cars had come along while she'd been unconscious and it didn't look as if there were going to be any more along this particular road today, in spite of the fact that it was still relatively early.

With snow falling this close to Christmas, perhaps

the locals were wise enough to stay at home with their families where it was warm and safe.

All she had to keep her company were memories, and they weren't going to be enough to keep her warm or get her out of there.

'How ironic,' she whispered. 'To spend a year trying to disappear only to be found every time, and when I *need* someone to find me, there's no one around.'

A solid kick landed on her ribs, as though to remind her of a certain person's existence.

'Apart from you, of course,' she apologised, stroking the spot with gentle fingers. 'But you're not really in a position to help.'

In fact, the ungainly shape of her body was the reason why she hadn't been able to reach the release for the safety belt; that and the fact that she didn't dare move too much in case she sent the car tumbling into infinity.

The fact that she could see her surroundings a little better led her to crane her neck towards the back of the car. She'd flung the two small bags that had contained all her worldly goods for the past year into the back seat when she'd taken off this morning. If they were within reach, perhaps she'd be able to get an extra layer or two of clothing to drape over herself while she waited for someone to find her.

There was one bag nearby, unfortunately the one with the tiny items she'd lovingly stitched and knitted in preparation for her baby's arrival.

'Perhaps I could put a mitten on each finger,' she mused with a watery chuckle, trying to fight off the first waves of real fear.

She knew that the rescue services always recommended staying with the vehicle rather than wandering off and getting lost, and she was wearing a thickly padded jacket, but that still left a large amount of her too poorly covered to preserve her body heat.

Over the space of a night, at these sorts of temperatures, she could soon be looking at the onset of hypothermia. And if the temperature dropped still further outside…

From her time on the neonatal ward, she knew only too well how critical temperature could be to tiny babies fighting for their lives. She had no idea what effect hypothermia had during pregnancy and was now praying fervently that she wouldn't have to find out.

She pulled the collar of her jacket closer around her cheeks so that the warmth of her breath was deflected down inside her clothing then tucked each set of fingers inside the cuff of the opposite sleeve.

'What if…?' she mumbled into the cocooning layer, slipping into a favourite childhood game.

Whenever Robert Wainwright had been at his most abrasive and domineering, she'd retreated into her own private make-believe world.

One of her earliest memories was of telling her favourite doll that she was really a princess and one day her father and mother, who were king and queen of a beautiful kingdom far away, were going to come for her, and then they'd all live happily ever after.

The scenarios had changed over the years, probably influenced by whatever books she'd been reading at the time, but one theme had remained constant.

Finding a way to escape the Wainwright sphere of influence.

How paradoxical it was that when she'd finally achieved her most enduring dream she should end up in such danger.

'But that doesn't mean that I can't imagine my way out of it,' she murmured, and set her imagination to work.

'If only...' Suddenly a pair of liquid silver eyes appeared in her mind's eye and it felt as if a hand squeezed around her heart. That was almost too easy.

'If only I hadn't had to leave Dmitri like that,' she whispered, feeling the hot press of tears behind her eyes. She closed them tight, refusing to give in to them. She knew she'd had no option when she'd seen that black car and recognised that all-too-familiar figure behind the wheel.

But in her game, Laurel could imagine that the car that had seemed to slow when it had passed the gateway a little time ago had been Dmitri's car.

She'd even imagined earlier on today that she'd seen the metallic sapphire of Dmitri's beloved sports car coming up beside her on the motorway, but by the time she'd looked again, all she'd been able to see had been nondescript saloons and high-sided lorries.

Anyway, there was no way it could have been Dmitri. It was so many months since she'd left him that he'd probably gone back to Russia by now and forgotten all about her.

But that couldn't happen in her fantasy.

In her mind she could imagine the way he'd see the damaged wall beside the road and instantly recognise it as the place where she'd tumbled down the hillside.

She could almost see him phoning for assistance then scrambling over the wall to help her out of the car and swear his undying love...

She snorted as her fantasy took off into the realms of impossibility. The last few years had left her with too few illusions about real life to be able to immerse herself in her make-believe world the way she had as a child.

'If only I hadn't left, I probably wouldn't even have been on that road at that time. I'd have been working on the ward and waiting to catch a glimpse of him...'

Another sharp jab in her ribs brought reality crashing through the fantasy.

Even if she'd been able to stay, she certainly wouldn't have been at work today, not at this stage of her pregnancy. She did a quick mental calculation of the number of days until her due date.

'Fifteen days to go, provided you arrive on time,' she murmured with a sudden burst of excitement at the prospect. She couldn't wait to hold her child in her arms for the first time.

Of course, the baby books all warned that first babies were notoriously slow to arrive, so she could still be waiting in a month's time.

'But only if I get out of here safely,' she said with a shiver of dread. She couldn't bear to think that, after all these months, she might never see the tiny being she'd been nurturing for so long.

'It's not going to happen like that,' she said, trying to sound positive, but even with her mouth buried inside the collar of her jacket she could hear the quiver in her voice. She ignored it.

'Any minute now, some kind person is going to catch sight of the damaged wall and is going to organise a rescue party. Then you and I will be taken to... Hey!' A sudden thought struck her. 'We'll probably be taken to the hospital at Edenthwaite to be checked over. I don't imagine there's one closer than that and I already know there's an accident and emergency department there.'

That information had been easy to find, unlike her sister's whereabouts. She'd moved about so often that it had been like trying to nail jelly to a wall, trying to pin her down. Even when she was standing face to face with her she wouldn't be certain that she'd found the right person. She hadn't been able to find out whether they were identical twins or fraternal, so she didn't even have the certainty that they'd look alike to go on.

'But when they're certain that you're all right,' she mumbled around a sudden jaw-cracking yawn, 'then I'll be able to ask if she's on duty, and ask to see her, and...and then...'

She was vaguely aware that she'd begun to ramble but it didn't really matter. The car was steadily getting colder and she was shivering hard enough to rattle her teeth, but her eyes were so heavy she just couldn't keep them open any longer.

It had been such a stressful day that she was tired out. Perhaps when she woke up her brain would be clearer and she could work out a plan...find a way to get out...

CHAPTER THREE

DMITRI raked his fingers through his hair as he waited for the call to be answered, marching impatiently up and down in the narrow space between the two beds in his hotel room. It felt as if he'd had the phone glued to his ear for hours.

'Hello? Can you help me?' he said, launching straight into his prepared speech. 'I need to know whether you have a guest called Laurel Wright staying with you. She would have arrived earlier this afternoon by car.'

'I'm sorry, sir, but we don't give out information about our guests,' said a snippy voice on the other end, and he could have groaned aloud. He could understand people's right to privacy but this was something different.

'She wanted me to join her,' he continued quickly, sticking to his improvised story and sure that the woman was going to cut the connection at any moment. 'I didn't think I'd be able to get away from work, but now that I have, I've discovered that I've lost the name of the place she's staying.'

'Hmm,' she said dubiously. 'That's as may be, but we haven't anyone of that name staying here, anyway. You said the name's Wright?'

'Yes. Laurel Wright,' he confirmed eagerly, not allowing himself to think that she might have booked in under another name. How would he ever trace her then? This was a phenomenally popular tourist area with hundreds of hotels and guest-houses dotted about, right down to the smallest farmhouse bed-and-breakfast. The fact that it was close to Christmas, rather than the high season between Easter and autumn, meant that many places would be closed, but he wouldn't know which until he asked each one individually.

'She's slim with long blonde hair and honey-coloured eyes,' he added hopefully. 'And she's got the most beautiful smile.'

'She sounds lovely,' the woman said, her tone almost sympathetic now. 'Unfortunately, she's not booked in here. We're not open for Christmas. Our next guests aren't due until around Easter-time.'

Dmitri thanked her for her time and rang off, only then giving in to the urge to swear ripely in his native tongue.

'This isn't getting me anywhere,' he said with a discouraged sigh. He wandered across to the window and gazed out into the brightly lit square.

There was a Christmas tree laden with coloured lights in the middle by some sort of monument and most of the buildings had decorations of some sort in their front windows. A few hardy souls were scurrying around with armfuls of shopping, their heads bowed to protect their faces against the whirling snow.

He felt a momentary pang of homesickness, then did a logical comparison between his home in Russia and this picturesque little town. This weather was relatively bearable, with temperatures just cold enough to freeze water where it lay. At this time of year in his home town he could be dealing with dozens of degrees of frost that could snap fingers off like dry twigs if he ventured too far without gloves.

People certainly wouldn't be loitering to admire the tree like that couple over there, the woman laughing at her male companion as she tried to catch a snow-flake on her tongue.

There was something about the light-hearted in-nocence of the game that made him look closer at her.

He'd grown accustomed over the last eight months or so to the momentary shock of seeing women who reminded him of Laurel. With one it had been the free and easy way she'd walked, with another the col-our of her hair or her spontaneous, slightly husky laughter.

With this woman it was…

Suddenly she turned to face directly towards him and his heart nearly stopped.

'Laurel!' he called out in disbelief when he saw the face he'd been searching for so long.

For several disbelieving seconds he stood trans-fixed by the sight of her, unable to drag his eyes away.

She was so beautiful.

How could he have forgotten the way she came alive when she laughed like that? It was almost as though there were another person hidden inside her, under her more serious professional side. A person she'd only become when she was with him…until now.

Suddenly he realised that she and her companion

had begun walking across the square together and he whirled towards the door.

He barely remembered to grab his coat and the key to his room on the way out and ignored the lift in favour of the stairs for speed.

His heart was pounding with a mixture of exertion and anticipation as he burst out of the hotel's main doors, scanning the rapidly whitening square as he thrust his arms into his sleeves.

'She's gone!' he whispered in disbelief when there wasn't a single person in sight, neither Laurel nor the man who had been with her.

It felt as if a hand tightened around his heart when he finally realised the significance of her companion.

He had spent months thinking about her and wondering why she'd left that way, while she... Well, it looked as if she'd blithely gone on with her life, forgetting him as if he'd never existed in the first place.

He closed his eyes against the sting that could only be caused by the whirling snow—it certainly couldn't be tears for a woman that fickle—and drew in a shaky breath. Reflexively, he wrapped his arms around himself, needing to do something to contain the pain inside.

It hurt, far more than he'd thought it would, and he finally had to admit that he'd been living on foolish hope. Against all odds, he'd somehow convinced himself that, when he found her, there would be some logical explanation for her sudden departure and she would admit that she'd missed him every bit as much as he'd missed her.

In his imagination, laughter and tears mingled as

she threw herself into his arms, vowing never to leave again.

He gave a snort of derision as he turned back towards the hotel entrance, suddenly aware of how cold and wet he'd become in spite of the milder climate.

He was halfway up to his floor when something inside him brought him to an abrupt halt.

'No!' he said fiercely, turning to make his way down again, a quick check telling him his car keys were still in his pocket. 'I'm not going to slink away without confronting her. Otherwise I'll never know why she went like that.'

It only took a moment to sweep away the thin layer of snow that had accumulated on his windscreen since he'd parked the car and then he was on his way.

'Denison Memorial, maybe,' he muttered as he followed the signs for the local hospital. He knew, from his laborious tracing over the last few weeks, that she'd worked at several hospitals, never staying very long in any job before suddenly taking off again. Perhaps the reason why she'd come to Edenthwaite had been to take up her next post. It would be easy enough to check, providing she was still using her own name.

He was pleasantly surprised when he caught his first glimpse of the hospital. It was far more modern than he'd been expecting, without looking in the least out of place in its surroundings. The fact that everything was highlighted by the lights gleaming across an untrampled layer of snow only made it look more picturesque.

As if he was interested in picturesque! he thought

grimly as he followed directions for the hospital manager's office.

The man's identity was a major surprise. The last time he'd seen him he'd been laughing down at Laurel while she'd tried to catch a snowflake on her tongue.

'Please, come in and take a seat. What can I do for you, Dr Rostropovich?' the man said when Dmitri had introduced himself.

'I'm hoping you can help me identify one of your staff,' he said bluntly, his heart heavy in his chest because he already knew the answer. 'I'm looking for Laurel Wright.'

He had to give the administrator his due—he'd barely blinked at the name.

'I'm sorry, but we don't have anyone of that name on the staff here,' he said politely. 'However—'

'But I saw her,' Dmitri interrupted brusquely, all too aware that his tone was almost accusatory. 'You were with her in the square in Edenthwaite less than an hour ago.'

Silently, the man held up a hand to silence Dmitri's outburst while he reached for the phone.

'Ah, Sister Fletcher, are you free for a moment?' he asked, then gave the sort of husky chuckle at her reply that hinted at a close relationship between the two of them. 'No, but I have a visitor here who would like to have a word. Five minutes?'

There didn't seem any point in indulging in small talk but Dmitri couldn't sit still, leaping to his feet to prowl backwards and forwards like a caged animal.

He hadn't expected the end of his quest to come quite so suddenly and his thoughts and emotions were in turmoil. Before she arrived it was time to put the facts he knew into some sort of logical order.

The man had referred to her as Sister Fletcher and, bearing in mind the hint of intimacy in his voice when he'd spoken to her and the fact that his name was Marc Fletcher, it would be safe to assume that Laurel was now married to him.

And in just a few minutes he was going to be face to face with her—the woman who had walked out on him all those months ago.

He still didn't know what he was going to say to her, and the problem was compounded by the fact that his replacement in her affections was going to be a witness to their meeting.

He whirled to face his silent observer and his pride was tweaked by the glimmer of humour he glimpsed in his otherwise steely grey eyes. It took more will-power than he'd expected not to give vent to the roiling feelings inside him. After all, it wasn't Fletcher's fault that he'd fallen for Laurel and married her. He wasn't to know that she'd left—

A brief tap at the door was all the warning he had and then she was there.

She walked into the room with a smile that could stop his heart, and very nearly did when he realised that it was directed at the man who'd straightened up from behind the desk as soon as she'd appeared.

His breath froze in his throat, her impact on him still so strong that he was glad he had the window-sill to lean against.

He would recognise the unconscious sexiness of that walk anywhere, and as for those honey-coloured eyes...he'd never forget the way they'd darkened when he'd taken her in his arms and kissed her for the first time.

'Lauren,' the administrator said with an answering smile as he rounded the desk to meet her. He wrapped a welcoming arm around her shoulders and when she would have reached up for a kiss, turned her towards Dmitri.

'We have company, Lauren,' he warned, although it was obvious to Dmitri that he had wanted to accept the kiss she'd offered. 'This is Dr Dmitri Rostropovich, who's come here looking for Laurel Wright. Doctor,' he continued, directing his words to Dmitri, 'this is my wife, Lauren Fletcher, née Scott.'

'You don't need to introduce us,' Dmitri said in a voice filled with gravel, ignoring what the man was saying as he fixed his eyes accusingly on hers. How could he ever have thought her trustworthy? 'Laurel and I first met over a year ago and we worked together on a daily basis until she disappeared suddenly about eight months ago.'

He'd felt betrayed when she'd left, but to see her here, like this, with *him*, made him feel as if his heart were being ripped out of his chest all over again. She was married and she had the nerve to smile at him as though everything that had happened between them was unimportant.

He'd always wondered why she'd left like that, especially after what they'd shared that night, but had been so certain that there would be a valid reason. He'd been so certain that she wasn't the sort of person who took pleasure in hurting others…or was she? There was no sign of penitence in her today. In fact, there was no sign of recognition at all.

The more he looked at her, the more changes he could see, from the shorter, flirty hairstyle to the new air of self-confidence that surrounded her even more closely than the administrator's arm around her shoulders.

'I'm sorry, Dr Rostropovich, but we really haven't met before,' she said, oh, so sincerely. 'You see—'

'Is not true!' he snapped angrily, foreign grammar going out of the window in a blaze of righteous anger. 'I understand you not wanting to tell your husband details of your life before you met him, but to…to resort to…to lies…' He flung his hands up in the air, conscious that his control over his accent was diminishing with every word, too. In a moment he'd be haranguing the woman in Russian.

'Dmitri, please! Listen!' she pleaded, her golden-brown eyes wide and liquid with the threat of tears. 'My name is *Lauren*, not Laurel. Laurel Wainwright—or Wright, as you know her—is my twin.'

'Twin?' he repeated blankly, the wind completely taken out of his sails for a moment while he grappled with a mental translation for the unexpected word. *'Bleezn?'*

'Please, won't you sit down?' she urged, turning a chair towards him, and he realised that he must look as stunned as he felt. He wasn't even sure that his legs would carry him that far. Why hadn't Laurel told him about her sister?

'Here,' a deep voice said as he slumped heavily into the welcome support, and he realised that a steaming cup of coffee had appeared in front of him, courtesy of Marc Fletcher. 'Or would you prefer something stronger?'

'*Nyet.*' He shook his head. 'No, thank you. This will be good.' He took a grateful mouthful in spite of its searing heat and it seemed to start his brain functioning again. He tightened his hands around the plain functional mug and dredged up the words to form an apology.

'I'm sorry for…for *that*. Please, forgive me, but I was so sure…'

'You aren't the first person to make that mistake,' Lauren said with a wry glance towards her husband. 'The likeness between us is very strong.'

'So, that wasn't Laurel but *you* I saw on the motorway this afternoon, driving towards Edenthwaite?' he mused aloud. He was suddenly utterly weary at the thought of all the checking he was going to have to do and all the miles he was going to have to drive to find out exactly where he'd lost Laurel's trail. For the first time he began to wonder if it *was* really worth the effort if she so obviously didn't want to be found. 'I was so sure…'

'No! It *wasn't* me,' Lauren said, sounding strangely excited. 'Are you sure it was today? She was coming towards Edenthwaite?'

'Positive. It was not long before the snow started. I glanced at the driver of a car I was overtaking and recognised you…*her*…and realised that I'd caught up with her purely by accident. I was only waiting for you…for *Laurel* to stop somewhere so I could speak to her when she suddenly turned off onto a side road. There was a…*gruzoveek*…a truck in my way so by the time I realised what she'd done I'd missed the turn and had to go to the next one and make my way back.'

'And you really think she was coming to Edenthwaite?' Lauren demanded, her eagerness almost a visible entity in the room.

'You tell me,' he countered with a shrug, puzzled by her intensity. He understood how much one could miss a family member during a long absence; it had been months since the last time he'd been to visit Babushka Ana. But nothing more than miles of motorway separated the twins, while his grandmother lived in central Russia. 'When were you expecting her? Is she coming to visit you for Christmas?'

'I've no idea,' she said with suddenly brimming eyes. 'We've never met. I didn't even know she existed until a few weeks ago and I've never even seen her photo.'

'Ouch! That hurts,' Laurel groaned when she opened her eyes some time later.

She felt strangely groggy and still quite stupid with tiredness—or was it the bump on her head? Perhaps she had concussion because, in spite of her uncomfortable position, all she really wanted to do was go back to sleep. Inside the car she was out of the wind at least, and it didn't seem to have got any colder, or was she just too tired to shiver any more?

She tried half-heartedly to move, but the crick in her neck that had woken her up gave her a sharp warning jab. Her ribs were aching and burning from the pressure of the seat belt but reaching the catch was totally impossible now. Unfortunately, the special gadget she'd bought to prevent the belt putting too much pressure on her belly during her pregnancy was now responsible for stopping her from reaching the release.

She didn't even want to think about certain internal pressures. After weeks spent running backwards and forwards to the bathroom, she knew only too well how limited her capacity was these days, and with no sign of relief in sight...

'I never thought I'd welcome the idea of a catheter,' she muttered, vaguely recognising that her words were as slurred as a drunkard's. She thought about trying to say it again, clearer, but the effort was too much.

Everything was too much.

Running and hiding had been too much.

Leaving Dmitri had been too much, especially when she'd had to leave her heart behind with him.

Coming so close to finding her sister, only to fail so ignominiously, was too much.

Sometimes it even felt as if living was too much...

'Ouch!' She dragged a strangely heavy hand across to rub the spot just under her ribs where a tiny limb had scored a direct hit.

The blow came again, this time landing almost in the palm of her hand.

Laurel closed her eyes against her surroundings as she concentrated on the sensation, realising anew that under her clothing there were only fractions of an inch between her hand and that precious little limb.

'I love you,' she whispered in a tear-filled voice as she wondered for the millionth time since she'd realised she was pregnant whether the tiny being they had created would resemble Dmitri.

Part of her hoped for it to happen. That way she would have a visible reminder of the only man she'd ever loved. But that was always countered by the fear that it would break her heart to see his features in the child every day, knowing that she'd lost the man who'd fathered it.

It?

She sighed, wishing now that she'd asked to be told the sex of the baby when she'd had that early scan. As it was, she'd just been relieved to see the tiny heart beating on the shadowy screen and marvelled that anyone could decipher the rest into arms and legs.

She frowned, remembering the appointment for a second scan that she'd never attended—how could she when, by that time, she'd moved on again? At least she'd been in a position to keep surreptitious track of her blood pressure in quiet moments.

Still, if her size was anything to go by, there was nothing wrong with the baby's development. She felt like a hippopotamus already and there were still two more weeks to go before her due date.

This certainly wasn't the way she'd imagined preparing for the birth of her first baby, trapped in a car in a snowstorm in the Cumbrian hills, half-suspended by a seat belt so she couldn't get comfortable.

She snorted. Get comfortable? She didn't think she'd been comfortable for months between the backache and heartburn and the gymnastics taking place inside her.

What she'd looked forward to, on those rare occasions when she'd dared to imagine her escape from Robert Wainwright, had been a husband at her side, waiting for the birth of their child as eagerly as she was. A man who would offer to rub her back when it ached, she thought with a grimace. A man who would lend her his strength to get out of a chair rather than see her struggling or, even better, fetch her a cup of tea to save her from getting out of the chair in the first place.

There was nothing she could do about the fact that, ever since she'd realised she was pregnant, her dreams had taken to putting Dmitri's face to that shadowy figure. She'd woken time and again to the recognition that it had been *his* hands she'd imagined soothing her aching back and tired feet and *his* arms she longed to cradle her as she tried to get comfortable at night.

She hadn't allowed herself to think about the impossibility of seeing him again one day, even if she did successfully complete her quest. That had been too painful.

As it was, she'd been convinced almost from the start that she was never going to find her twin, at least not in time to thwart Robert Wainwright's plans.

Not that it had stopped her from searching, following up every lead, grasping at every straw.

It had been a major boost to learn from her mother's letter that she and her sister shared such similar names. It had taken much longer and, she had an uncomfortable feeling, had taken some marginally illegal manoeuvres to uncover the names of the couple who had adopted her. After all that, it had been exasperating to find out that they'd died, leaving her twin to the none-too-tender mercies of the state system.

A long-ago memory of a girl who had befriended

Lauren in a foster-home had supplied the clue that her one-time friend had wanted a career connected with medicine.

Laurel had marvelled at the coincidence that had led the two of them into such similar lives. Unfortunately, she'd never realised just how long that was going to take to research. So, here she was, a year on and much closer to her goal, but not quite close enough.

And still too late for any success with her quest to make a difference with Dmitri.

Even if she'd found her sister months ago, it didn't mean that Dmitri would have been hers for the taking. So much time had passed now that his sabbatical year would have ended. He was probably thousands of miles away in Russia again.

Besides, she thought sadly, the way she'd had to leave him almost guaranteed that he wouldn't want anything further to do with her. The scant note she'd left had been more for her benefit than his.

Her eyes closed as if there were lead weights on the lids and her thoughts seemed to be getting slower and slower. Still, the thought of being so tantalisingly close to Edenthwaite was enough to make her cry with bitter frustration. Better by far to think about those first happy days after she'd met Dmitri. Then, working in the same department had been a joy, no matter how many sour looks Melanie Richards had sent her way, and life had seemed full of possibilities.

'Have you eaten yet?' Dmitri had demanded as she'd emerged from the cloakroom a couple of days after their first meeting with her uniform stuffed in a plastic bag for the journey home.

'Dmitri!' she'd gasped, startled to find him apparently waiting for her, then had realised what she'd said. 'I'm sorry, I should have said Dr Rostropovich.'

'Dmitri is better,' he'd said decisively, reaching for her arm to guide her towards the nearest exit, as though her compliance had been a foregone conclusion. 'We are not on duty now, with Sister Richards glaring at us, so we can be more friendly.'

'But...' She'd subsided. How could she have argued with him when she'd been thinking of him as Dmitri almost from the moment she'd met him?

'So, have you eaten yet?' he demanded as they went out into the early darkness of the December afternoon.

'No. I was going to pick up a pizza on my way home.'

'Pizza? *Moosar!* Is rubbish to fill you up,' he declared dismissively. 'You come with me and I will give you good Russian food. *Azoo.*'

'*Azoo?*' she repeated warily, even as she was fascinated by his unexpectedly boyish enthusiasm.

'Is small pieces of meat in a sauce. Rich sauce. Thick and tasty from being cooked a long time and smells... Ah! *Choodyesni*...wonderful!'

She couldn't help laughing at the fervent way Dmitri kissed the tips of his fingers.

'And where are you going to find this *choodyesni azoo*?' she quizzed, mimicking his pronunciation and hoping she'd got it nearly right at least. 'Is there a Russian restaurant around here?'

'Better than any restaurant,' he declared with a

proud lift of his chin and a gleam in those fascinating silvery eyes. 'I cook it myself.'

Laurel couldn't turn him down because she didn't want to. There was just something about the man that she found impossible to resist, not least because he was the first man who had ever offered to serve her a meal prepared with his own hands.

'Oh, you were right,' she groaned a little while later when she put the first steaming bite into her mouth. 'This *azoo* is definitely *choodyesni*. You must have trained as a chef as well as a doctor.'

'Not a chef. Babushka Ana taught me when I went to live with her,' he said softly, and she saw the shadow that took the vibrancy out of his eyes for a moment.

'*Babushka?*' she repeated, the word sparking a memory from her childhood. 'Isn't that the word for all those wooden dolls that fit inside each other? I was given one as a gift once.' Not that she knew what had happened to it. It had disappeared when she'd been in hospital one time, and no one had seemed to know where it had gone.

'Sometimes they are called *babushka* and sometimes *matroshka*,' he agreed, 'but Babushka Ana was my...my father's mother,' he finished, apparently temporarily stuck for the word.

'Your grandmother?' Laurel supplied, fascinated by this tiny glimpse into his background. 'Why did you go to live with her?'

Instead of answering, he pressed his lips together in a thin line, his face losing its animation as though he'd been somehow turned to stone. Suddenly she realised that she'd asked him to talk about an unhappy time, but before she could offer to take the question back he began to speak.

'My father was a soldier. A good soldier,' he said softly, with the echo of a young boy's pride. 'But there was an accident with a big gun…a *vzrev*.' He mimed.

'An explosion,' she whispered, hoping that by supplying the word she wouldn't interrupt his story.

'Yes. An explosion. And because there were not enough doctors to help him, a good soldier never came home again.'

Laurel didn't have to imagine how devastated Dmitri had been. It was all there in his eyes.

'Then, when my mother became ill and had to go to the hospital, Babushka Ana came for me and took me home with her.'

She had no right to ask—she barely knew the man, for heaven's sake, no matter how much she wanted to—but she had to know what happened.

'And then?' she prompted, knowing there was more from his withdrawn expression.

'My mother died,' he said quietly. 'I think her heart was broken. And Babushka Ana…she is dying by *dooe*.' He held his hand up with an infinitesimal space between his finger and thumb. 'Alzheimer's disease,' he finished hollowly.

'Dying by inches,' she murmured, knowing just how apt that description could be. And if Dmitri was the last surviving member of his family…she could only imagine how bereft he must be feeling, especially so far from home.

'It is too late for her now, but in the early days of

her illness, when she knew what was happening to her and that there was no cure...'

Emotion robbed him of words for a moment and Laurel could only marvel at the strength of will that helped him to recover and continue. The significance of the fact that he was revealing so much of himself to someone he'd known such a short time was something she was going to have to think about later.

'She told me not to waste my energy on grief for her,' he went on in a husky voice, the eyes that met hers full of clear conviction in spite of the grief. 'She said I should use it to do good for others. That way, fathers will not bleed to death and one day no one will have to watch their *babushka* die by inches.'

And he had taken her words so much to heart that here he was, a doctor specialising in taking care of the most fragile new lives and living thousands of miles from the last precious member of his family in the quest for more knowledge.

It took her a moment before she could be certain that the threat of sympathetic tears wouldn't show in her voice.

'And you honour the other things she taught you by cooking *azoo*,' she pointed out with a slightly shaky smile.

'Not just any *azoo*,' he objected, after half a beat taking his lead from her and acting affronted. 'This is *choodyesni azoo*.'

CHAPTER FOUR

'How can she have disappeared into the air?' Dmitri demanded, his nerves raw with frustration. 'I travelled along that same road and there was not a sign of her.'

'How much traffic did you see?' Lauren asked. 'If she changed her mind at the last minute—got cold feet about meeting me, or something—you might not have seen the car coming in the opposite direction because you weren't expecting it. Or perhaps she turned onto a side road.'

'*Nyet*. She would not do this. She was coming to see you—her twin. Anyway, it was beginning to snow quite hard on this smaller road and I only saw one car coming the other way—a black car, big and heavy like Russian government cars.'

'A big black car?' Marc repeated with a glance towards his wife. 'That sounds horribly familiar.'

'Robert Wainwright's car?' Lauren guessed. 'He was certain I was Laurel but once we convinced him otherwise, I was sure he'd gone back home again. Do you suppose...?'

'Heaven only knows,' Marc said grimly, reaching for the phone.

'Who is Robert Wainwright and what does he have to do with Laurel?' Dmitri demanded when he couldn't stand trying to follow the incomprehensible conversation any longer.

'You'd better explain, Lauren,' Marc said as he

waited for a connection. 'I'm phoning the police to see if they've heard anything useful.'

Lauren beckoned Dmitri across to the chairs on the other side of the office and perched on the arm of one.

'Robert Wainwright is Laurel's adoptive father and he's been trying to track her down ever since she left home about a year ago.'

'Track her down? But why would he want to? She's twenty-eight years old now, and has her own life.'

Dmitri rubbed both hands over his face while he tried to make sense of this latest information. Laurel certainly didn't need her father to take care of her. From what he'd learned about her life when they'd been working together, because of her adoptive father she'd had to become very good at taking care of herself.

And anyway, if she'd wanted someone to take care of her, he would have been only too willing.

'We haven't yet been able to find out anything definite so we've been trying to read between the lines,' Lauren explained. 'From what we've seen of him, he's a very domineering person and he's got some special reason for wanting her to go home with him. He even hinted that she's been on medication for a psychological problem.'

'*Moosar!*' he exclaimed, then translated when she blinked. 'This is rubbish! She is a qualified nurse in a demanding neonatal ward. She doesn't need drugs to lift her up or bring her down.' More than that he didn't like to tell them without Laurel's permission.

Even as he said it a worm of doubt began to nibble

away at his certainty. Could her sudden disappearances be evidence of that psychological problem, or had her father prompted her flight each time?

'Well, he's been pretty determined to find her and take her home,' Marc said when he came across to join them.

'To the point of making a complete nuisance of himself when he thought *I* was Laurel,' Lauren said. 'The only good part was that when the police were checking up on his story and comparing it with mine, they came up with the information that we were twins, each adopted by a different family soon after we were born.'

'Now Lauren's just waiting and hoping that Laurel makes her way here so they can finally get together,' Marc continued. 'The police just confirmed that they've had no reports of any major accidents or anyone stranded in the snow. They've got their usual patrols out and they've promised to let me know if the situation changes.'

'And in the meantime…' Dmitri said with a heavy sigh, fighting against the feeling that he must have missed something important on his way between the motorway turnoff and Edenthwaite.

'In the meantime,' Lauren finished for him, 'as far as we know, Laurel has either stopped somewhere for the night or her father has found her and taken her home whether she wants to go or not.'

'I should have booked somewhere to stay for the night,' Laurel muttered into the eerie quiet that had descended when the wind finally died away. 'Then someone would know I'm missing.'

As it was, there was no one in the whole world who was worrying about her safety…except, perhaps, Robert Wainwright. And if he was worrying about her it would only be because she could ruin all his plans.

She gave a harsh chuckle at the thought.

All those years that he'd had to put up with her while he'd waited for her mother to die; years when he'd deliberately undermined her at every opportunity until she'd honestly begun to doubt her own sanity, not knowing that she'd been little more than his hostage.

She'd never know what it was that had prompted her to volunteer her time at the local children's hospice.

It could have been something as selfish and mundane as the desire to get away from Robert Wainwright for a few hours at a time. She would prefer to think that it had been something that had come from her heart; that she'd just wanted to do something to ease the difficult and sometimes far too brief lives of the children who'd stayed there.

That had been the start of a dramatic change in her own life, starting with an innocuous conversation over an early-morning pile of hot buttered toast with the resident psychologist.

The grandmotherly woman would never know how far-reaching her words had been. Later that day Laurel had spent time with a formulary investigating the various tablets she'd been taking on a daily basis for so many years.

It had taken two years to wean herself off them to confirm her suspicion that she didn't need any of them and probably never had.

She would always wonder what sort of tale her uncle had spun her GP to secure the first prescription because, as far as she could remember, he'd been a kindly man and most unlikely to over-prescribe for the sake of it.

Many times during those hard-fought two years she'd been glad that she'd decided to pretend to be continuing with her medication as usual. It had lulled Robert into believing that he wouldn't have any problem maintaining his control over her, even when she'd been accepted to start her nursing training.

She'd been in her final year when he'd told her that as she would be getting married in the New Year there was no point in continuing with the course. It had taken a private conversation with her future husband, Robert Wainwright's ambitious assistant, and the threat of refusing to marry him to secure his support for continuing, at least until she'd finished her training.

It had been pure chance that had put that vital letter into her hands, just weeks before the wedding, and had precipitated her flight. It had been several months later that she'd caught sight of a newspaper article that had mentioned the company her family had built over several generations and which Robert Wainwright had supposedly been managing on behalf of his wife and her sister.

The rumour in the paper had suggested that there was a possible merger afoot between the family-owned company and their much bigger competitor, but the deeper she'd probed, the less she'd liked what she was finding.

How strange it had felt to be on the outside looking

in and having her first clear view of what had been going on in her life.

Suddenly, several questions that had been puzzling her for years now made sense.

She'd known for a long time that her adopted mother's marriage hadn't been happy—how could it have been when she'd been barely allowed to speak in her own home? But as her husband was responsible for the financial security of the whole family, and the prosperity of the company, she'd been trapped.

As for her own position, it was only now that Laurel realised that the cocktail of tranquillisers poisoning her bloodstream had been Robert's long-term insurance policy that, once her real mother died, she'd meekly sign the papers that would at last give him overall authority.

To confirm her suspicions she'd needed an impartial source, and a visit to an internet café had netted her the information that the details in her mother's letter were accurate. Far from being Robert Wainwright's company, as he had implied all her life, he had only married into the firm. And now it seemed as if he had found a way to sell the company and pocket the proceeds, if he could get her to sign on the dotted line.

Her mother's letter had also given chapter and verse of the way she'd been forced by family pressure to give up her illegitimate child for adoption by Robert and his wife. Unfortunately for Robert's plans, the letter also spelt out the fact that she'd never told her family that there had been two babies born that night, not one.

Once Laurel had realised that she had a sister, the

wording of her mother's will had told her just how imperative it was to find Lauren before Robert discovered she existed.

If Lauren didn't know about her connection to the company, she wouldn't realise the significance of the proposed merger—that Robert Wainwright was expecting to receive an obscene amount of money for delivering her family's company to their competitor. Unless her sister knew the background that Laurel had uncovered, she wouldn't know that the company she now part-owned was in danger of being the victim of a notorious asset-stripper who would put hundreds of long-time employees out of work to satisfy Wainwright's greed. Laurel certainly wouldn't put it past the man to resort to trickery to get Lauren to sign her share over to him.

All Laurel had to do was find her sister and explain the situation to her before Robert got there first, and she'd come so close to succeeding.

Not only that, but she'd been within a few miles— definitely less than five—of meeting the other being with whom she'd shared a mother's womb.

So near and yet so tantalisingly far away.

And if she didn't get rescued…soon…perhaps she'd never have the chance to find out if they could have been friends.

She'd read so many books since she'd discovered the existence of her twin, wanting to know as much as possible about the almost magical phenomenon.

Once she'd established the fact that her 'other half' was still alive she had actually dared to wonder if there was a chance they would develop that myste-

rious communication system that other twins sometimes did.

A stray gust of wind whistled around the car, buf-
feting it a little even as it blew drifts of delicate ice
crystals against it.

Suddenly, Laurel was afraid.

The wind might have dropped but those delicate
flakes were still falling steadily. Supposing it snowed
all night? Supposing there was so much of it deposited around the car that, even if someone thought to
check the road she'd travelled, they wouldn't see her?

It had been several days since she'd mentioned a
possible 'Christmas break' to a neighbour, speculating idly on the charms of Cumbria, but she doubted
whether the woman would worry about her until the
New Year.

Whoever had been trying to follow her on the motorway in that big black car had lost her long before
Edenthwaite had appeared on the signs.

So, realistically, there was no one in the whole
world who knew where she'd been making for, or that
she'd turned off onto this secondary route in an attempt to disguise her destination from any pursuers.

Her fear escalated as she forced herself to accept
that it could be a long time before anyone found her
here—or, at least, found her in time before she suc-
cumbed to the cold.

Laurel drew in a sobbing breath and the muscles
in her back gave a twinge of complaint. Unfortunately, when she breathed out again, the pain didn't
go away. Instead, it grew stronger and radiated around
her sides until it met at the front, right under her hand.

In horrified fascination she felt the swell of her

belly harden until the whole of it was completely rigid under her trembling palm.

'No! Not yet!' she ground out through clenched teeth, praying frantically that this was just another episode of Braxton-Hicks' contractions. She closed her eyes and concentrated on relaxing, deliberately counting as she breathed in and out, slow and even.

'Relax,' she instructed herself, consciously unclenching her hands and trying to direct her thoughts down less stressful avenues.

If only she could learn to switch off, the way Dmitri could. Perhaps it was something doctors had to learn if they were to survive their training—the facility for shutting down their brains and sinking into sleep at any opportunity.

It seemed so long ago now, but she could remember the first time she'd come across him slumped in a chair with his long legs stretched out in front of him, his arms folded across his chest and his head twisted uncomfortably to one side.

Laurel had been surprised when Melanie Richards had actually chosen *her* to fetch him, until she'd realised that her superior had already had the parents of one of their newest patients waiting to speak to her.

She'd paused a moment, hating to wake Dmitri after the day he'd had. She'd known he'd been exhausted after spending time with the distraught relatives of a patient they'd just lost to necrotising enterocolitis. Then, before he'd had a moment to recharge his batteries, or even grab a cup of tea, they'd had another emergency transfer of a critically ill baby born to a methadone addict.

The last thing he'd needed had been to be woken

out of a deep sleep to deal with yet another emergency, but she'd had no option. The patient had been due to arrive in a matter of minutes and he needed to know what was coming.

She reached out a hand to touch him, undecided for a moment whether she dared to stroke his face the way she wanted to, or shake his shoulder the way she should.

She could imagine what his jaw would feel like, with the dark shadow of his emerging beard lending him a slightly piratical air. She knew that he had warm hands even on cold days because she'd heard him telling the parents of one of their more fragile charges when he'd needed to touch the infant.

He'd laughed when he'd told them, telling them that it was because he was a hot-blooded Russian and throwing the words out with a glance in Laurel's direction almost as if they were a challenge. Would his jaw be warm, too, or chilled from staying so still in this little-used room?

She was still leaning towards him, trying to make her decision, when his eyes opened to stare straight up into hers.

'*Ahnghel,*' he murmured in a drowsy voice, and reached out towards her.

Mesmerised by the look of wonder in his eyes, she didn't think of moving away as he stroked his fingers over the loose strands of hair that had escaped the French braid she'd fashioned so many hours ago.

The electric sensation that shivered through her when he drew those exploring fingers around her jaw was enough to bring her to her senses.

'D-Dmitri, there's another patient coming in just a

moment,' she managed in a shaky voice, completely forgetting to straighten away from him.

He blinked once, long eyelashes veiling his eyes for a second, then he was focused.

'What details?' he asked briskly, while she stepped back and mourned the loss of his touch.

'Respiratory infection. He's a transfer from a domino unit, somewhere in Cumbria, who weren't confident they had the expertise to deal with a problem preemie,' she explained as she watched him trying to stretch the kinks out of his back.

His shirt needed tucking in at the back and his tie was hanging at half-mast, both of which he rectified, apparently unaware of her fascinated gaze, but his hair was as adorably rumpled as if he were a little boy getting up from a nap.

'How old is he? Do you know what they've done for him so far? Have they identified the organism responsible?' he prompted, all sleepiness obviously banished.

He grabbed his jacket and slid one arm into a sleeve, already off with that long-legged stride towards the ward. She almost had to run to keep up, breathlessly filling in the details she knew, at the same time wondering why he was bothering to put the jacket on at all. She could almost set her watch by the length of time it would take him to get rid of it once he'd introduced himself to the parents of his new charge.

He shrugged his shoulders to settle the jacket comfortably over them, then at the last moment remembered to drag his fingers through his hair to restore it

to some sort of order, but she could still relish the
sleep-rumpled image left in her mind.

'Adam Kersley,' Dmitri confirmed from the notes
that had arrived with him. 'Ten days since delivery
at thirty-five weeks gestation.'

'He was just a bit snuffly a couple of days ago,'
his distraught mother butted in, wringing her hands
with fear for her baby. 'We thought he might have
caught a cold from one of us but he just got worse
and worse until...' She broke off as sobs overtook
her.

'Mrs Kersley,' Dmitri said, stumbling slightly over
the unfamiliar combination of letters in her name. 'I
promise I will do everything I can for Adam, but you
must do something for me.'

'Anything!' she vowed fervently, and Laurel saw a
wry smile quirk the corner of Dmitri's mouth.

'I will hold you to that!' he said seriously. 'Now,
I want you and your husband to go to the cafeteria
and—'

'No! We want to be here with—' she began frantically, only to go silent at the unspoken admonish-
ment of Dmitri's upraised finger.

'You promised!' he reminded her. 'Now, *we* are
going to be getting Adam settled into the unit and
taking some samples from him for analysis while *you*
are going to be eating a proper meal and drinking at
least two glasses of fruit juice.'

'But—'

He ignored the interruption this time, continuing
inexorably. 'You are already exhausted with worry
because your baby arrived early, and it is going to be
several days before you will be certain that all is well

with him now. He will need you to be strong and healthy to help him, and you cannot be strong and healthy if you don't eat properly.'

They both had concerned expressions on their faces and looked as if they would still like to argue, but when they nodded their agreement Laurel knew his words had reached them.

'I will see you back here in two hours,' he directed as they cast a last longing look at their precious child, and when Mrs Kersley opened her mouth to object to the time limit, he merely lifted that finger again to remind her of her promise.

'Now, we need to get busy,' he said as soon as the door closed behind them. 'I want a sample of naso-pharyngeal secretion and five mils of whole blood for serology, heparinised for viral isolation. Get them up to the lab as soon as possible.'

'Then you'll know what's the matter with him?' Laurel asked as she hastened to provide the necessary equipment.

'I'm almost certain that I know now,' he murmured softly as he listened to the tiny chest again, then pulled a face at what he heard. 'I think it's RSV—respiratory syncytial virus.'

Lauren heard the word 'virus' and her heart sank.

'Is it very bad? He won't die, will he?' she demanded fearfully. She hadn't been working in the department long enough to even start becoming accustomed to losing her tiny charges—didn't know how anyone *could* become accustomed to it.

'If it were a normally healthy older child or adult, he would be able to get better in about nine or ten days without treatment.'

'But because he's premature…?'

'We're going to have to give him some help with ribavirin.'

Laurel had heard of the drug before. 'That's an antiviral drug, isn't it?'

'Exactly. It will help to stop the virus from reproducing, so that his lungs won't be overwhelmed by the infection before he can fight it.'

'How long will that take? He's already struggling to breathe.'

'His lungs don't sound good,' Dmitri admitted sombrely. 'And as he was early, they are one of the weakest parts of his system.'

'But the ribavirin can clear that up fairly quickly, can't it?'

'Like most drugs, it also has side effects,' he pointed out. 'It can cause the breakdown of red blood cells, leading to anaemia, and with a system as tiny as his…'

Little Adam wheezed as he tried to cough and didn't even have the breath to cry.

'He'll need more oxygen, too,' Dmitri muttered under his breath, and Laurel silently passed him the tiny mask she'd already reached for, pleased that she'd been able to anticipate what he was going to say.

Hopefully Adam would do well enough with oxygen support not to need to go on the respirator.

Across the other side of the room a monitor sounded its shrill warning and with a hurried, 'I'll be back,' Dmitri strode across.

'Poor Kai,' Laurel murmured, able to see even from that distance that the tiny scrap was having another convulsion. The fact that his mother had been on methadone right up to the time she'd come into hospital for his delivery was the reason why he was having such a hard time. It didn't help that he was an addict's typical small-for-dates offspring who probably had a host of developmental problems still to be revealed.

The irony was, if his mother had still been on heroin, Kai would probably already be over the worst of his acquired addiction by this stage. It usually only took three or four days of treatment with phenobarbital or chlorpromazine before the drug would have largely left his body.

Even though it produced similar withdrawal symptoms, the same couldn't be said of methadone. Instead of several hours after birth, it could be seven to ten days before the agonies of withdrawal started, and they could go on for anything up to six weeks. It could be several years before the long-term effects of the addiction on the development of the child's central nervous system would be known.

'Even with intramuscular Valium his muscles are rigid,' Dmitri muttered angrily when he came back to check on Adam.

It was several hours later, when she went to take her break, before Laurel spoke to Dmitri again.

'Tea?' she offered when she had plugged the kettle in and washed a couple of mugs out. She'd actually been slightly dubious about saying anything when she'd seen the way he was frowning. But perhaps the offer would draw him out of his dark thoughts.

'*Prasteet-ye?*' She'd clearly startled him when she'd spoken. He'd been so preoccupied that he hadn't even heard her come into the room.

'Tea?' she repeated, hoping there wasn't a problem with his grandmother. It must be very difficult for him with so many miles between them.

She was just leaning towards him to hand him one of the mugs, wondering if she dared to offer a friendly ear, when he suddenly burst into speech.

'I just don't understand,' he exclaimed, throwing his hands up in disgust and nearly knocking both mugs of tea out of her hand.

'*Eezveeneet-ye!*' he exclaimed, hurrying to steady them for her with one hand under the mugs and the other on her wrist. 'I am sorry, Laurel. Did you get burned?'

'Not a drop,' she said with a shaky smile, and let him take one of the mugs before she sat down.

It wasn't the hot tea but the contact of his hand on her wrist that had seared her nerves, but she had no idea *why* it was happening. She hadn't felt anything like it before, not even with the man she'd been engaged to. Now it was almost as if the slightest contact between the two of them completed some sort of high-powered electrical circuit.

'What don't you understand?' she asked, needing to get her brain working properly again.

'How Kai's mother could carry on taking the drugs even though she *knew* it was dangerous for her baby. She even took another dose just before she walked into the hospital, knowing she was in labour.'

'She told me she's been on hard drugs since she was fifteen,' Laurel said. 'It would have been hard for her to give up.'

'Even if it is a matter of life and death?' he demanded heatedly.

'If she's too addicted, she wouldn't even have thought of that,' Laurel pointed out. 'Even if she's managed to come off heroin and onto methadone for her own sake, she probably didn't realise that it actually makes withdrawal worse for her baby.'

Dmitri just grunted, obviously irate, and she wondered at his clear antipathy. Was there something in his past that had made him so apparently unsympathetic to someone addicted to drugs?

Her empathy was based on her own history, even though she'd never been seduced by hard drugs. Perhaps if she told him…

'It is such a waste!' he snapped. 'A waste of her life and a waste of money, usually gained from breaking the law, just to "escape" from the realities of life.'

His tea slopped dangerously close to the rim of the mug as he gestured then he turned those intense grey eyes on her. 'You sound as if your sympathy is for Kai's mother, but a hard life is no excuse for what she is doing. Babushka Ana had a hard life but she didn't "escape" with vodka or cigarettes or drugs, and she never broke the law. She needed every penny for food and heat, especially when she brought me to her home.'

Laurel was silent, smarting after such a resounding rebuff, then heard him sigh heavily.

'I'm sorry, Laurel. That was rude,' he apologised in a low voice. 'It's just…she says she loves Kai and yet she wasn't willing to do this one thing for him before he was born. And if she was like this for her pregnancy, what about all the months and years while he is growing up? Will she "escape" from feeding him and clothing him just so she can satisfy her own cravings? No. I cannot understand this way of behaving.'

'That's because you've never been addicted to something,' she said quietly, staring down into the remainder of her tea while she pictured her own struggle. She *could* empathise with Kai's mother because she still felt ashamed of what she'd been like in those days, even though she knew that it hadn't been her fault.

Dmitri was such a strong person, physically and mentally, that he probably *wouldn't* be able to understand how it could have happened, but...

Suddenly she made the decision to tell him. She was a different person now, but she'd only become what she was today because of what she'd gone through.

'Dmitri, for much of my teenage years I was on a cocktail of tranquillisers and antidepressants,' she confessed in a low voice. She barely dared to watch him out of the corner of her eye because she was so certain she would see the shock appear on his face.

She should have known that he would have far too much practice at keeping a poker face to betray a reaction.

'You're not taking them now?' It was worded as a question, but his tone was far more positive—almost an affirmation of his confidence in her that warmed her to her soul.

'No, I'm not,' she confirmed. 'But, Dmitri, I *was* seriously addicted to them after all that time. It took me nearly two years to wean myself off them.'

'You were lucky. Some people cannot kick the

habit, they are so addicted. You had professional help?'

'No help at all. The opposite, in fact. My father was actually checking up on me to make sure I *was* taking my tablets. I ended up resorting to throwing more and more of them down the toilet each day as I gradually cut my doses. I'd started volunteering at a children's hospice so it was harder for him to check up on what I was doing.

'Then, once I was certain that I had kicked them completely, I applied to start my nursing training.'

It was probably far more than he'd ever wanted to know about her, and was far from the full story that had brought her to this place and this time, but she did have a point in baring her soul like that.

'But that is wonderful!' he exclaimed, making no attempt to hide his delight. 'To have the determination to go through all the...' He paused for a moment, searching for the elusive word he wanted. 'Withdrawal symptoms,' he finished triumphantly. 'Were they very bad?'

'Yes,' she admitted bluntly, and then drove her point home. 'But probably *not* as bad as it is for Kai, or as it would be for his mother.'

He blinked, suddenly realising where the whole conversation had been leading, then grinned wryly and angled his head in a nod of acknowledgement. 'I concede,' he admitted with a heavy sigh. 'Perhaps, because I can see what would be best for other people, I'm guilty of expecting them to see it too, especially when it involves one of our little babies.'

'Perhaps,' she agreed, inwardly delighted that he'd been big enough to make the concession. Some of the doctors she'd met since she'd embarked on this career had egos far too fragile for that sort of humility. 'It's too late to make any difference to Kai now. We'll just have to hope that his mother is one of those who realises what her lifestyle would do to him in the future and makes the effort to change.'

She'd had a concession of her own to make the following day when Kai's mother, a painfully thin young woman who barely looked as if she was out of her teens, cornered Laurel when she was coming out of the staff lounge.

'That foreign doctor frightened me,' she admitted quietly. 'I didn't realise how bad Kai would be, or that you wouldn't be able to take all the pain away from him.'

Big tears welled up in her china-blue eyes and Laurel instinctively put a supportive arm around her bony shoulders to lead her to the nearby interview room.

In view of the number of painful talks that went on between the four walls, there was always a box of paper hankies sitting on the little table by the two-seater settee.

'Would you like a cup of tea, or coffee, perhaps?' Laurel offered when the young woman had mopped up a little.

'Yes… No. Actually, I wanted to know…is there a drug-rehab place somewhere near the hospital?'

'You want to know if there's one nearby, or you want a place in one?' Laurel asked, deciding there was no point in beating about the bush.

'I want a place in one,' she said firmly, if a little shakily. 'It might not look like it when you see what

I've done to him with the methadone, but I love my baby and I'm not letting Social Services have an excuse to take him away from me.'

'It'll be hard,' Laurel warned bluntly, drawing from her own experience. 'Probably the hardest thing you've ever done, because the determination to succeed has all got to come from inside you.'

The younger woman was obviously afraid but the way her chin came up and her shoulders squared gave Laurel a feeling of hope. 'I don't expect it to be easy, but it'll be worth doing it, for Kai.'

'Definitely a battle worth fighting,' she agreed. '*You'll* be taking charge of your life, rather than letting expensive chemicals in your bloodstream do it.'

'So, how do I find out about rehab programmes? I want to start as soon as possible—I've wasted enough of my life.'

Laurel had promised to make some enquiries and get back to her as soon as she could, but couldn't help making uncomfortable comparisons with her own life. She looked back all those years to the zombie-like days of her own addiction, and then made herself focus on the responsible job she was holding now. Where would she be in another five years?

'Hopefully, not still looking over my shoulder,' she muttered as she set off for the unit again, wondering who would have the information she needed.

CHAPTER FIVE

YET, here she was, nearly a year later, still looking over her shoulder, knowing that Robert Wainwright was desperate to get her under his control again, Laurel thought wearily.

At least Kai's mother had followed through on her determination to do something about kicking her drugs habit. Having her baby taken away from her would be held over her head the whole time, but hopefully that would be enough incentive for her to see the rehab through to the end.

Then, perhaps, she could start to make some plans for the future.

In the darkness Laurel pulled a face. At this rate, the young woman would reach her goal sooner than she herself would. Whenever she thought she was making some progress, another hurdle appeared in her way. At least she didn't have to worry about the baby for a while. Her knowledge of anatomy and the working of the body's systems were enough to reassure her that it would be warm and safe inside her. She would have to lose a lot more heat before it affected her core temperature.

At least that last contraction had only been another Braxton-Hicks' in preparation for her delivery in another couple of weeks. She didn't like to think what she would do if she were to go into labour before someone found—

Laurel didn't even have a chance to finish the thought.

Without any warning, there was a sudden gush of fluid as her waters broke and, with the realisation that she really was in labour, terror swamped her.

'Dear God, please, send somebody to help,' she sobbed, hardly able to catch her breath as a powerful contraction tightened inexorably. 'Anybody…even Robert Wainwright.'

That thought was enough to make her shudder, even as the pain began to ease.

After the things he'd put her through, she dreaded to think how he'd treat her illegitimate child, but if it was a choice between the man she'd spent the last year evading, or death…

It would probably mean she would never have a chance to meet her twin. With her innocent child as a hostage she would have no option but to obey his every dictate, signing on the dotted line where he told her to and keeping her mouth shut over the fact that they both knew she was not legally entitled to do so.

The only way to avoid that situation was if someone else found her first—a passing motorist, a shepherd out with his dog—anyone who would help her to contact her sister.

Another contraction began to tighten its grip on her and she cried out in fear. One part of her had been counting on the fact that first labours were usually slower than subsequent ones, but with contractions this close together it wasn't going to be long before she and her baby were in serious trouble.

'Lauren!' she shrieked when the pain reached such

a pitch that she felt as if she was being wrenched apart.

'Please... Please, help me, Lauren. I need you...' she wailed helplessly when it finally began to ebb.

Dmitri couldn't remember when he'd felt so helpless before.

He could remember feeling lost when he'd seen his mother being taken to the hospital, but he'd known that Babushka Ana would come for him. Then, he'd known with absolute certainty that Babushka Ana would always be there for him, scolding, guiding, loving.

The blow of realising that she'd been turning into someone else entirely, and the loss that had struck him the first time she'd called him by his father's name, with no recollection that *he* existed at all, had been no less devastating, but they had been taken with the fortitude of a grown man.

That fortitude seemed to have deserted him completely with the uncertainty over Laurel's whereabouts.

In his mind's eye he kept seeing the blinding whirl of snowflakes caught in his headlights as he'd been driving towards Edenthwaite. He was certain Laurel couldn't have had the same amount of practice at driving in snow as he had—few people in England would have experienced the depths of a Russian winter.

She could have turned off the road somewhere to stop for the night. There was no way of knowing if she'd taken refuge in one of the tiny one-room bed-

and-breakfast establishments that didn't even bother advertising beyond a painted board at the roadside.

But what if she wasn't settled cosily in front of a warm fire? What if she'd been disorientated by the movement of the crystals and had driven off the road by mistake? What if she'd lost control in the icy conditions?

A sudden sound from the other side of the room snapped him out of his fearful imaginings.

'What's the matter, Lauren?' Marc demanded, clearly concerned for his wife.

Dmitri could see she'd gone quite white and strode across to see if he could help.

'I don't know what's going on but…did you hear something?' Lauren asked, her eyes darting around the room.

'What sort of thing?' Marc had knelt beside her chair to hold her hand. 'The wind's dropped a bit but it's still snowing. Did you hear it against the windows?'

'Not that. It was a voice,' she argued, and turned to Dmitri. 'Did you hear someone calling?'

'What sort of voice? What did it say?' Long practice had Dmitri trying to draw information out of her rather than denying what she was claiming. Arguing with distraught parents when their tiny baby's life hung in the balance was a complete waste of everyone's time and energy.

Not that he would have classed Lauren as distraught, but she *had* been under a great deal of stress recently.

'It was a woman's voice,' she said, the distant expression in her eyes telling him that she was concentrating on replaying the sound in her head.

'Do you recognise it? Is it a voice you know well?' he prompted.

'No... I'm not sure.' She shook her head and closed her eyes tightly. 'But there's something about it that... She was calling my name.'

Suddenly her eyes flew open and she was staring wildly from Marc to Dmitri and the expression sent a shudder up his spine.

'It's Laurel!' she gasped. 'I'm sure it is.'

'*Laurel?* But...' Marc began, but she wasn't listening. She'd already leapt to her feet and was hurrying towards the door, grabbing her coat as she went.

'She's in danger. She needs help,' Lauren declared with utter conviction as she stepped out into the corridor. 'I've got to see if I can find her.'

Dmitri was on his feet in a flash. He didn't know whether there was anything to Lauren's premonition or whether it was just her fear for her twin's safety that was making the suggestion. What he did know was that he'd had enough of waiting and wondering.

The biting cold stung his face as he emerged from the hospital to trek across the snowy car park. It was a good job he remembered where he'd parked because all the vehicles looked the same under their blankets of white.

'How are we going to organise this?' Marc called over the top of his four-by-four while Lauren shut herself into the passenger side and tightened her seat belt impatiently. 'Shall we take opposite sides of the road and explore all the possibilities?'

Dmitri spared a brief smile for the evidence of

Marc's military training. He remembered that his own father had always liked to be well organised, even for something as simple as a shopping trip.

'Fine,' he agreed easily, grateful that they were finally doing something. 'Have you got a mobile phone so we can keep in contact?'

They exchanged numbers and set off into the alien snow-covered world.

An hour later frustration was beginning to set in.

Even if Laurel *had* pulled off the road, the snow had been falling so steadily that any tracks would have been covered long ago.

At first, Dmitri had driven down each cart track, regardless, terrified that if he missed one, it would be *the* one that led to Laurel's whereabouts. It had taken him a while to realise that she was just as much a stranger to the area as he was and would be unlikely, in deteriorating weather, to go exploring unmarked lanes.

That had still left miles of road to travel *en route* to the motorway junction he'd seen her use, progress painfully slow as he investigated any snow-covered vegetation or pile of rocks that even vaguely resembled a car.

'*Pazhalsta*, she is safe somewhere,' he said fervently as he climbed back into the car. Somehow, the reality of this search was completely wiping out his previous anger towards her. His own pain at the way she'd left was nothing in comparison with the fear that she might be out here somewhere, in danger.

Before he could drive on again his phone rang and his heart lifted.

'Hello? You've found her?' he demanded as soon as he heard Lauren's voice on the other end.

'Not a sign. How about you?' She sounded really discouraged, and he wondered how much effect this was having on her conviction that she'd 'heard' Laurel calling her.

'Nothing,' he admitted, frustrated by their lack of success. 'Where are you now?' He pinpointed his position in a tiny lay-by on the map.

'Marc's suggesting that we need to compare notes so we're not duplicating our efforts,' Lauren relayed. 'Stay where you are. We'll be with you in five or ten minutes.'

While he waited for Lauren and Marc to join him he took a moment to look around him from the warmth of the car.

The snow had gradually eased off and while the sky was still dark with clouds, there was an unearthly luminescence that belied the late hour.

Up here, high above Edenthwaite, there was barely a sound beyond the soughing of the wind across the hills. Even in daylight there would be little to see at this time of year beyond mile upon mile of thin stony grassland broken only by the snaking criss-crossings of stone walls.

What trees there were had been stunted and mis-shapen by the bitter winds at this altitude and, this late in the year, there wasn't even the bleat of a sheep for company.

He shuddered at the thought of being stranded in such a place and his concern for Laurel mounted.

*   *   *

Desperation over the last hour had forced Laurel to find a position to give her baby at least a chance of life after delivery.

She was still terrified that the car might tip over the edge of a precipice but she'd managed to squirm far enough around within the confines of the seat belt to wedge her shoulder against one headrest while she braced a foot against the other. She had no idea how long she was going to be able to hold the position but at least it would allow her to reach down to support the emerging child until it was fully delivered.

Whether she would be able to withstand this level of pain and still be able to think clearly enough to control the delivery was another matter, and one she didn't want to think about. Neither would she allow herself to contemplate the possibility that there would be any complications.

'Distraction. That's what I need,' Laurel said aloud.

The fact that the car windows were now completely covered by snow was making her feel distinctly claustrophobic and as for her rapidly escalating labour...

Unfortunately, the only thing that came readily to mind was Dmitri and how desperately she wanted him at her side.

She knew how impossible it was, in the circumstances, but she'd always assumed that the father of her child would be with her for the birth of their child.

The next best thing to having him there was to remember the last time she'd seen him, the day she'd realised that Robert Wainwright's bloodhound had tracked her down again.

She would always regret that she hadn't explained why she'd had to go; she certainly hadn't intended it to happen that way. In fact, she'd actually gone to his

flat specifically to tell him that she was going to have
to leave, but once he'd opened the door, all her care-
fully prepared speech had disappeared like smoke in
a winter gale.

'Laurel,' he'd murmured hoarsely when he'd seen
her standing there, apparently undecided whether to
invite her in or not.

'Dmitri? Are you all right?' She'd stepped forward
when she'd caught sight of his reddened eyes, her
own concerns forgotten. 'Has something happened?
Is it your grandmother?'

Silently, he'd widened the door to invite her in.

'Oh, Dmitri,' she'd murmured, wrapping a com-
forting arm around him as easily as if she'd been doing it for years. What had her own problems mattered
in the face of his distress?

'I didn't realise she was so ill,' she'd continued
softly as she'd led him to the large comfortable armchair provided with the room. 'When did she die?'

'She didn't die,' he'd said in a choked voice as
he'd slumped into the chair. He'd threaded his fingers
between hers and held on as if she'd been his lifeline,
bringing her to perch on the arm of the chair.

She was looking down on his head while his gaze
was focused on their joined hands as he continued.

'I was speaking to her…by telephone. I phone her
every week but this time…' He shook his head and
the tear that fell on their joined hands was her first
indication of the depth of his misery. She'd never
known a man to cry before.

Uncertain how to react, she waited silently for him
to regain control, marvelling at this unexpectedly
emotional side of him. Apart from brief flashes of

wicked humour, he always seemed so self-controlled and eminently polite on the ward, his emotions reserved for his tiny patients and his part in their struggle for life.

'I was speaking to her, but she was speaking to me as if I were my father,' he said roughly, sounding as if he had gravel in his throat. 'I tried to tell her that he was dead and that I was her grandson but she just got more and more agitated.'

'Oh, Dmitri,' she breathed, taking a chance on being rebuffed as she slid her free hand around his shoulders for comfort. She knew that his Babushka Ana was his only relative. What must it be like to lose the only person you'd known and loved all your life?

'It was the first time this happened,' he explained, tilting his head to look up at Laurel with his long dark eyelashes all clumped together in vulnerable spikes by his tears. 'The first time she hasn't known me...treated me as if I'm someone else.'

They both knew that this was part of the progressive nature of Alzheimer's disease and marked a deterioration in her condition. She could still have years of physical health ahead of her, but once that spark of recognition had been for ever extinguished, how much worse it must be for those left behind.

As if he were one of their bereaved parents, mourning the loss of a child who had just lost the fight for life, she found herself stroking Dmitri's shoulder in an attempt to offer comfort.

'Ah, Laurel, I'm sorry,' he sighed, tilting his head to rest on her shoulder. 'Is selfish to cry, but if she is gone then I have no one.'

Part of her grieved for his approaching loss but part of her also envied him the years of love he'd received. From the way he'd spoken about his Babushka Ana, it was obvious that they were very close.

She rested her cheek on his head and felt her heart break a little more. It was the first time in her life that she'd dared to care for someone. Now that it seemed as if he needed her as much as she needed him, how could she bear to leave him?

'Don't apologise,' she whispered shakily, the threat of tears almost preventing her speaking at all. 'I'm glad I could be here for you.'

'Ah, *ahnghel*,' he murmured, and his hand cradled the back of her head as he looked up into her eyes. '*Spaseeba*…thank you for being here…'

He tightened his grasp until his lips touched hers for the first time, briefly, lightly.

It was nothing more than a benediction—a symbol of gratitude for her understanding—until he drew back and met her eyes.

She didn't know what he saw there but with a groan he reached for her again and pulled her across his body until she was wrapped tightly in his arms.

This time the fleeting warmth of mouth on mouth quickly burst into a conflagration that roared out of control to consume them both.

It had been several hours before Laurel had woken in his bed, their bodies still intimately twined around each other.

Her first thought was of how much she loved this man, and her second of how much she was going to miss him, especially now that they'd…

She gasped when she caught sight of the clock, the

illuminated numbers telling her just how many hours had passed since she'd arrived to tell him she had to leave.

She didn't regret a single one—how could she when they were all and more than she'd ever imagined? But she couldn't help worrying whether this precious time had lessened her chances of escaping Robert Wainwright's clutches.

Dmitri was so soundly asleep that he barely stirred when she slid out of his embrace. Remembering the highs and lows of emotion he'd gone through in one evening, it was hardly surprising that he was exhausted, she thought as she hurried into her clothes.

Unable to bear the thought of leaving without some sort of farewell, she grabbed an empty envelope from the waste-paper basket beside his desk to pen a brief note.

She vaguely noticed that it had Russian stamps on it, but her heart was so full of all the things that she wanted to say that it was hard to know where to begin.

In the end, all she could do was stick to the two most important points.

'I love you. I'll miss you,' she wrote, unhappy to discover that she'd already started crying when a tear splashed onto the words.

She didn't dare look back at him as she tried to prop the note somewhere he would find it as soon as he woke. Then there was no more time to lose. She needed to put as many miles between herself and Robert Wainwright's bloodhound as she could.

She could barely drive for the tears streaming silently down her cheeks. Only the thought that she had to stay ahead of those who would try to take her back kept her going. To thwart Wainwright's greedy plans, she *had* to find her sister.

Then, if it hadn't taken too long, maybe she could come back to make the explanations she should have gone into last night...if Dmitri was still willing to listen to her.

Except her search had taken so much longer than she'd expected, especially once she'd discovered that Lauren had run away from a questionable foster-home and had apparently disappeared into thin air.

Another contraction built to a crescendo and she couldn't help shrieking through gritted teeth.

'Help me. Please, help me,' she wailed, shivering as the frigid air met the sweat that broke out on her body with each fresh wave of pain.

How much lower was the temperature going to drop, for heaven's sake? It was already far too cold for a newborn to survive, even with the small store of clothes she'd managed to drag out of her sparse belongings, and if she took off any of her own to wrap the child...

She racked her brain, trying to think of another solution, but there was only one to hand. With her fingers crossed that the tumble down the hillside hadn't done damage to vital parts of the engine, she reached out to turn the key in the ignition.

She held her breath as she made the connection, terrified that she might be about to cause an explosion. The fact that the exhaust might be covered by the drifts of snow, forcing carbon monoxide back into the car, seemed a relatively minor complication by comparison. Perhaps she could run the engine for a few minutes at a time, just long enough to warm the car without risking a build-up of the deadly gas.

She knew she wasn't thinking very clearly any more, but one thing she did know—if her baby survived the trauma of an unassisted birth to a woman dangling from a seat belt in a crashed car, she didn't intend it to freeze to death.

If only she'd bought the mobile phone she'd thought about soon after she'd set off on this quest. It would have been a wonderful way of calling for help as soon as the accident happened, but she was beyond worrying about that now.

'If the pains get much worse, they'll probably hear me shouting all the way in Edenthwaite,' she moaned as another contraction began.

Dmitri wound down his window part way to clear the condensation that was beginning to collect on the windscreen.

With just the ticking of the cooling car for company, he was more conscious than ever of the isolation of this spot. The sharp bark of a dog…or a fox…echoed around for a brief moment, but the snow seemed to be deadening even that noise far sooner than it should.

Somewhere in the distance he heard the sound of an engine and glanced at his watch. It was far too soon for Marc to have travelled so far. There must be another car on the road nearby. Perhaps it was someone who lived locally, someone who might know where a beautiful young woman and her car might have disappeared on a snowy December night.

When the sound remained steady he realised he

must have been mistaken. Had it been another car it would have passed him by now. Could it be a generator, supplying energy to a nearby farm that had lost power?

The noise of a second engine joined the first and this time it *was* Marc and Lauren, who soon glided to a halt behind him.

He wound up his window and climbed out of the car to join them in the four-by-four.

Dmitri didn't know what made him pause as he climbed into the other car. With one foot on the high-clearance running-board he steadied himself with one hand on the top of the door and straightened to his full height to look out across the surrounding area.

From this vantage point he could see that, beyond the stone walls bordering each side of the road, the land fell away on both sides, almost as though the road ran along the top of a ridge.

It still amazed him that every stone of these countless miles of walls had been gathered and crafted by hand centuries ago. The farmers who maintained them now were, in all likelihood, the direct descendants of those original craftsmen.

Earlier in the day he'd noticed that there were sometimes large isolated boulders left in the enclosures and he'd imagined the original workers shaking their heads over the impossibility of moving them.

There was one such monolith in the field beside them, for example. Because of the slope of the hillside it had been invisible from the vantage point of his own car, even though the top of the wall at the roadside needed to have several rows of stones replaced.

He couldn't help speculating a little about the reason for the disrepair. Had the stones been dislodged by sheep trying to scramble from one pasture to another in search of grass or shelter from a storm? Perhaps their fall had been the result of natural disintegration due to their exposed position, or maybe some more serious mishap?

'Have you seen something?' Lauren called from inside the car, and for a second he felt that deep instinctive reaction to the woman who looked so like Laurel.

He flicked a last glance towards the hulking shape further down the slope. How many thousands of years could a boulder like that survive the weather up here before it eventually crumbled into dust? More than he could imagine with his mind so full of their frustrated search.

'All I can see is far too many miles of snow-covered rocks and grass,' he sighed as he ducked inside the vehicle and closed the door against the biting cold.

Marc had his map spread out on the console between his seat and Lauren's, and Dmitri leaned forward to run a finger over it to trace the area he had covered.

'I just don't understand it,' he said when he finally straightened up, running a frustrated hand through his hair yet again. 'There's nowhere for her to stay and she certainly wouldn't have decided to sleep in the car in this weather. Anyway, her car might be nondescript grey, but we'd still have seen it if she'd pulled in somewhere with car trouble.'

That was one of the advantages of such a wind-swept area. There were few areas of vegetation lush enough to hide anything more than a huddle of sheep, unless you descended into a sheltered gully fed by a stream. Even then, the ubiquitous sheep would have nibbled any greenery off the stunted trees as far as they could reach.

'It felt as if she was afraid of something far more serious than car trouble,' Lauren said sombrely, then grimaced an apology. 'I'm sorry. That sounded as hokum as one of those stage fortune-tellers, and I've no idea where it's coming from.'

Dmitri saw the consoling hand Marc laid over her white knuckles and was struck by a bolt of envy that stole his breath.

That was what *he* wanted—that sense of connection that didn't need words—and he'd had an uncomfortable suspicion for the last eight months or more that it was *his* fault that he'd lost out on the possibility with Laurel.

The more he thought about it, the more he believed that it must have been his wariness...his reticence to talk about his deepest feelings...that had driven Laurel away. If he'd been able to put into words all the things he'd been feeling...

But what would have been the point? It would all have had to finish the same way in the end, only with *him* being the one who left *her*. He had obligations in Russia that had to take precedence over any softer emotions, no matter how compelling.

'Babushka Ana—my grandmother—would say that the heart knows more things than the mind,' he said to Laurel. 'Outside the cities, people are far more accepting of such things. That is especially true for the connection between twins.'

'But it's crazy to think that I could have any such connection with Laurel,' Lauren protested. 'I didn't even know she existed until a few weeks ago. We've never even met.'

'Not since you were born, but the heart knows more things than the mind,' Dmitri repeated. 'And if you *have* suddenly developed some sort of telepathic connection, then I wish you'd tune into it again to tell us what we're missing.'

'I don't know anything more than I told you before, back in Marc's office,' she said with a discouraged grimace. 'I just had this overwhelming sensation that she was in some sort of danger and she's terrified.'

'So all we can do is keep looking until we find her,' Marc declared as he folded the map to a more convenient size then met his wife's worried gaze. 'And we won't stop *until* we've found her, I promise.'

With their new search areas allocated, Dmitri was just climbing out of the vehicle again when he realised that the night seemed even quieter than before.

He lifted his head to listen, trying to work out what had changed. There was something missing. Something had changed since he'd climbed into Marc's four-by-four.

'The generator!' he exclaimed when he finally realised what was different.

'What generator? Where?' Lauren quizzed over the back of her seat, and he felt guilty when he heard the sound of hope in her voice.

'It's not important,' he said, leaning back into the warmth of the car to reply. 'It's just that while I was waiting for you, I could hear a generator running nearby. The farmer must have switched it off while we were talking because I can't hear it any more.' He straightened up to tap the top of the vehicle. 'Good luck with your search. Keep in touch. If you see *anything…*'

Even as he was speaking he heard someone trying to start the generator again. It had failed to fire for the third time before he registered what he was hearing.

'That's not a generator! It's a car!' he exclaimed, as he stepped up onto the running-board again, twisting this way and that as he tried to pinpoint the direction the sound was coming from.

There was absolutely no reason why it should have anything at all to do with Laurel, but at this moment they had nothing better to go on.

With a feeling of disbelief he realised that the sound was actually coming from the rocky monolith he'd spotted part way down the slope of the pasture beside them. It wasn't until there was a sharp bleat of a car horn—the sort of noise made when it was sounded by accident—that he finally realised what he was looking at.

'There's a car in that field! It's on its side,' he called back over his shoulder as he leapt to the snowy ground and took off towards the nearby gate.

Behind him he could hear the doors opening and knew in the back of his mind that both Marc and Lauren were following him, but that wasn't what he was concentrating on.

Suddenly, as though the occupant of the car had only just realised that the horn could be used to attract attention, there was a series of long, desperate-sounding blasts.

CHAPTER SIX

ANOTHER pain was trying to rip her in half and Laurel had to stop pressing the horn. Anyway, she couldn't concentrate on anything other than what her body was telling her to do, everything inside her focused on bringing new life into the world.

The urge to bear down was so overwhelming that she barely registered the moment when the door above her was wrenched open, showering her with snow.

Her eyes tight shut with the effort of pushing, she was only peripherally aware of voices, male and female, and of hands reaching to support and comfort while the pain lasted.

Light played over her tightly closed lids so she knew her rescuers could see the full extent of her predicament. Suddenly, for all the intensity and immediacy of her advanced stage of labour, she had the sensation of security and protection. She knew that she could concentrate on giving birth because others had taken over caring for her.

The contraction was beginning to fade when she felt someone climb into the car with her, someone lithe enough to slide past her into the back of the car without difficulty.

A female voice quickly relayed the information that she was trapped as much by the ungainly shape of her body as by her seat belt.

Then arms were reaching through the door opening and strong hands were gripping her under her arms. Another pair was waiting to take the weight of her legs when her mystery companion located the seat belt. By the time the contraction finally died she'd been released and was ready to be hoisted up onto the side of the car.

'It's all right, Laurel, we've got you,' said a soothing voice, and she looked up into the face of a complete stranger.

'Thank you,' she panted, then closed her eyes briefly while she caught her breath. It was funny that now she knew there were people willing to help her nothing seemed so bad, not the cold and snow or the prospect of delivering a child in the middle of a field.

Then a warning bell sounded in her head.

'Who are you, and how do you know my name?' After all she'd gone through, had she fallen into Robert Wainwright's scheming hands again?

'He's Marc Fletcher and he's a doctor,' said the female voice, as slender hands passed out the last of her scant belongings and prepared to climb up out of the stricken vehicle. 'He's also my husband.'

'But…' That explained half of her question but still left a big hole in the other half—or had she missed something? The next contraction was building but she didn't think her brain had completely shut down. 'How could he possibly know who I am?'

'Because we were looking for you,' the woman said as she dropped to the ground and turned to face her. She angled the torch she'd been using in the car so that it illuminated her own face—an eerily familiar

face. 'Hello, Laurel. I'm Lauren,' she said with a suspicious hitch in her voice.

Laurel didn't know what to do first.

Her body was telling her in no uncertain terms that
it wanted to get that baby out *now*, but all she could
do when she should have been pushing to assist the
contraction was stare in disbelief at her twin's face.

'Can we do the introductions later?' growled the
man with his arms wrapped around Laurel's shoulders, and when she heard the accented voice that had
haunted her dreams for all those months she was convinced that the whole scene must be some sort of
hallucination.

'No!' she groaned in despair as she closed her eyes
and concentrated on pushing the child a bit closer to
the end of its journey.

Logically, she could see why this was happening.
She'd been on her way to find her sister, so that would
account for her presence in the delusion, but she'd
left Dmitri so long ago and so far away. The last
person she would expect to find on a snowy fellside
in Cumbria was the darkly intent Russian she'd lost
her heart to all those months ago.

The voices were busy around her again, but this
time she was determined to ignore them. They
couldn't help her give birth to her baby. She was going to have to gather her wits and do that all by herself.

'At least imaginary people can't do me any harm,'
she muttered when she could spare the breath, and
heard an unexpected chuckle.

'We're not imaginary,' the woman said cheerfully.

'Laurel, I promise you, we're going to get you out of here and into a nice warm delivery room.'

'I'll believe it when I see it,' she muttered, still totally unconvinced that she wasn't making up the whole conversation, then gave a shriek when she was suddenly swung up into a pair of strong arms.

'Believe,' commanded a husky voice right by her ear, but it was hard. She'd never expected to hear the strangely seductive way Dmitri had of pronouncing the simplest word.

Before she had any more than a glimpse of that leanly aristocratic face another contraction was on her with the speed and force of an express train.

As if he knew exactly how she felt, Dmitri stopped briefly on his trek up the snowy slope.

'Can you pant, Laurel?' he asked in a coaxing tone, his voice close to her ear and apparently completely unaffected by the weight of the burden he was carrying. 'Just until we get to the car. We need to check that it's safe for you to push.'

'*You* can pant,' she snapped, the urge to push far too strong to be denied even though one part of her brain could see the logic of what he was saying. 'I'm getting this baby out as quickly as possible.'

How he managed to negotiate the rest of that snowy slope without jostling her, she'd never know. All she did know was that by the time the contraction eased they were at the open back of a powerful four-by-four.

'You drive. I'll get in the back with her,' Dmitri ordered as three pairs of hands swiftly manoeuvred her into the dimly lit space.

'What about your car?' Lauren asked, the direction

of her voice telling Laurel that she was getting into the front of the vehicle.

'I'll come back for it later,' Dmitri said dismissively as he joined her in the back to kneel at her feet. 'Let's get going. Now.'

Dmitri flicked a last glance at the vehicle he was leaving behind.

The lay-by wasn't much more than a wide place in the road but, provided it didn't get completely snowed in, the car should be safe enough there.

Unlike the woman in front of him, who might not be all right if they didn't get her to Denison Memorial as quickly as possible.

Disbelief still had his heart beating so hard that he felt slightly sick.

He'd been determined to find her, but never in his wildest dreams had he imagined that their reunion would be like this. He'd thought his emotions had been affected when he'd seen Lauren, but that was nothing to the knowledge that this was Laurel, his Laurel, and that she was having a baby.

Whose baby?

His?

Did the dates add up?

Did it *matter* whether they added up?

Laurel groaned as they hit a bump and the sound snapped him out of his trance.

What did the paternity of the child matter when she needed help?

'Another contraction coming?' he asked, leaning forward to take the extra jacket Lauren was holding out towards him then wrapping it around Laurel's chilled body. 'Do you want us to stop?'

'They keep coming,' she moaned, rolling her head from side to side, then snatched an extra breath and began pushing.

'How's she doing?' Marc called from his seat behind the wheel. 'I'd rather get her to the hospital, but if she'd rather stop when she's pushing...'

'Don't stop,' she gasped as she drew in another breath. 'Baby's early. Want it in hospital.'

Dmitri's emotions were on a roller-coaster ride.

Baby's early, she'd said, but that told him nothing when judged against the size of the tautly swollen bulge where her slender waist had once been.

Did she mean that it had been conceived in the months since she'd left him and would need the special skills of a neonatal unit? If so, were they travelling in the wrong direction? Did she need to go to the city hospital rather than Denison Memorial? Would there be time to get there before the baby was born? Unlikely, if she was already in advanced second stage labour.

He knew far too much about all the things that could go wrong with very premature babies to want to deal with one in the back of a car. Even a hospital with no neonatal facilities wouldn't be a good option, and he had to force himself to wait until the contraction eased before he asked the question burning his tongue.

'How early is it?' he demanded gruffly, dreading the answer.

'Two weeks,' she panted, and he allowed himself to relax a little. At least the child should be developed enough to survive without too much intervention. For the moment he refused to allow himself to think about what it meant on a personal level.

They'd reached the outskirts of Edenthwaite now, and the streetlights were painting her with broad bands of orange light, illuminating the wisps of blonde hair that had escaped confinement to frame her head like a halo.

The light might be intermittent but there was plenty of it for him to see the shadows under her eyes and the underlying air of strain that had little to do with the ordeal she was going through at the moment.

The one thing that was painfully obvious, especially with her hands rhythmically stroking it, was the bulge of the child she carried.

Whose child?

The thought broke through in spite of his best efforts. He was desperate to ask, but this was neither the time nor the place to confront her. He was going to have to wait until the delivery was over and they didn't have an audience.

Courtesy of Lauren's mobile phone, there was a reception committee waiting as they pulled up outside the accident and emergency department.

'The lift is ready and waiting to take you up to the domino unit,' a voice informed Dmitri as he settled Laurel gently in the waiting wheelchair. She seemed frighteningly frail for a nearly full-term mother.

'We put out a call for Jack Lawrence,' the voice continued over his head, 'but he warned that it'll be twenty to thirty minutes before he gets here.'

'Jack's one of Denison's GPs,' Marc explained in an aside, obviously for Dmitri's benefit. 'He special-ised in obstetrics and gynaecology before he did his GP training.'

Dmitri wasn't interested in the specifics of the arrangements as long as something was being done for Laurel. The baby he could deal with himself.

To satisfy the primitive protective instincts raging through him he would rather have carried her all the way to the delivery room than put her in the waiting wheelchair, but hospital protocol dictated otherwise.

'Provided there are no complications, we can manage without Jack,' Marc promised as Dmitri set off, pushing the wheelchair towards the lift yawning open in readiness.

'Which midwife is on duty? Katy, Faith or Lissa?' he heard Lauren ask.

'Lissa's on duty but Katy hadn't yet left to go home when your call came through,' the unknown voice said. 'They're both getting everything ready.'

Dmitri hit the button as soon as he entered the cubicle and Lauren had to put on a last-minute spurt as the lift doors began to close so that she didn't get left behind.

He was unapologetic. Courtesy wasn't a consideration, with Laurel alternately gritting her teeth and panting through yet another contraction. All he was interested in was getting her up to the delivery room as soon as possible.

There were two young, fresh-faced women waiting to take over pushing the chair as soon as he appeared, but he growled something unforgivable at them and kept going. Luckily his lapse in manners had been delivered in basic Russian and had only left them with puzzled expressions.

It was the same situation—minus the epithets—when it came to examining Laurel. To spare everybody's blushes as they stripped the rest of her cold, damp clothing and performed a quick examination, he positioned himself at her head, but he was determined that he wasn't leaving her side, not after trying for so long to find her. And as for the child…

He switched off the thought and concentrated on watching the two midwives going about their tasks, pleased to see that their quiet competence was unruffled in spite of his eagle-eyed presence.

'The delivery is too close to warrant attaching the foetal monitor,' one of them said in an aside to him as Laurel strained through another contraction. 'She's already crowning.'

'She is?' A cold shiver snaked its way up his spine at the realisation that she'd come so close to disaster. If she hadn't accidentally sounded the car horn, he and Marc would have driven away just seconds later to begin their search elsewhere.

'Did you want to see?' one of the pair asked cheerfully.

'You're not squeamish, are you?' the other chimed in quickly. 'We don't want to have to pick you up off the floor if you pass out. There won't be time.'

He managed a dry chuckle. 'I'm a doctor. I won't pass out.'

'You'd be surprised!' she countered with a roll of smiling blue eyes. 'It wouldn't be the first time it's happened. There's something about the emotional impact of watching your child coming into the world that seems to override mere logic.'

Watching your child coming into the world…

The words had the impact of an explosion in his heart, even though he couldn't be sure.

Suddenly, he needed to be sure; needed to know, in that earth-shattering moment, that it *was* his child.

Instead of taking the young woman up on her invitation, he turned to face Laurel squarely for the first time, deliberately waiting for her to open her eyes at the end of the contraction so that he could make contact.

Her face was sheened with sweat and blotchy with effort, but she'd never looked more beautiful to him. In that moment, all the anger he'd fostered over the interminable months since she'd disappeared seemed so petty...something to be dealt with another day. Even knowing who had fathered her child became an irrelevance with the realisation that *he* was the one here with her for the birth.

And then her eyes opened and she looked straight up at him as if she'd known that he'd be waiting for her.

'Oh, Dmitri, you're really here,' she whispered, her honey eyes full of tears. 'I honestly thought I was imagining you.'

He had to swallow before his voice would work.

'You always had a vivid imagination,' he growled, and saw her eyes light up at the memory the words brought back.

'How is Sabaka?' she demanded.

'Is that what you're calling the baby? Sabaka?' piped up one of the midwives, reminding both of them that they had an audience. It didn't stop them laughing.

'Hardly!' spluttered Laurel, then had to take a deep

breath as the next contraction took all her concentration.

'It means "dog" in Russian,' Dmitri was left to explain, but the words were automatic. His attention had been captured by the fact that, as the contraction built, Laurel had reached for his hand as though it was the most natural thing in the world, and was now squeezing it as if it was her one lifeline.

He couldn't believe that they could so easily slip back into that easy communication they'd discovered together. How could it be that, all these months later, they could share the same thoughts, laugh at the same memories. It was almost as if they had never been apart.

'Sabaka's fine,' he said with a smile, remembering when she'd believed that the dog's name sounded exotic. It had almost seemed as if she blamed him personally for the fact that it meant something as prosaic as 'dog'.

That had been the first time that he'd accused her of having a vivid imagination.

'In fact, she's better than fine since she added the children's ward to her round.'

It had been Laurel's suggestion that the patients in the geriatric department would benefit from the fairly new idea of pet therapy. The proposition had been prompted, in part, by the sad-eyed stray who'd narrowly escaped death near the hospital gates and had been adopted by one of the hospital porters.

The fact that he'd gone to bat for her with the hospital authorities had been rewarded by the first spontaneous hug she'd ever given him and almost immediately a marked improvement in the mood on the ward, even in some of the Alzheimer's patients.

From there it had been a fairly short step to promote a visit by the gentle creature to the children's cancer ward.

'You managed to persuade the hospital to allow it!' she exclaimed, and he suddenly remembered that the hospital's agreement hadn't come through until after she'd left.

There wasn't time to comment because with the next contraction and a groan of success that seemed to be dragged all the way up from Laurel's feet, the infant's head emerged.

'Laurel, listen, now. I need you to pant for me while I check that everything's safe. You mustn't push until I make sure the cord isn't in the way,' one of the midwives ordered.

'But I want to *push*,' Laurel wailed. 'I want to see my baby.'

'You concentrate on panting and I'll help you see the baby,' Dmitri bargained. 'Come on, pant like Sabaka!'

She chuckled weakly but complied while he slid an arm around her shoulders and lifted her high enough to catch a glimpse of dark hair plastered flat against a tiny skull.

'All clear, Laurel,' came the call as he laid her back again, this time with his arm around her shoulders. 'You can push as soon as you like.'

His knuckles were being ground together by the strength of her grip, but Dmitri watched in fascination while first one shoulder then the other was guided out into the world, swiftly followed by a slither of limbs.

'*Malcheek*,' Dmitri murmured, feeling the tears of joy begin to tumble down his cheeks as he turned to Laurel. 'Is a boy,' he repeated hoarsely, just only re-membering in time to translate.

As he looked down into the face of the woman he held against him, he saw that Laurel was shedding tears of her own. Suddenly he was seized with the impulse to declare his love and realised that it was the same overwhelming feeling that had nearly over-come him the night the two of them had first made love...the *only* time they'd made love.

'Katy, I think we've got a problem,' he heard one midwife mutter hurriedly to the other, and anything he might have said to Laurel had to be forgotten.

'A problem?' he repeated.

Fear filled his heart in an instant as he raked the naked pink infant with a frantic gaze. He was cer-tainly crying loud enough that his lung capacity wasn't in doubt.

'What's wrong? What's the matter with him?' Laurel demanded shrilly, struggling to see.

'*Nothing*'s wrong with him. He's perfect,' Katy re-assured them as she hurriedly wrapped him in the waiting warm blanket and brought him over. 'Here you are, Mum. You can count all his fingers and toes for yourself.'

Laurel was completely diverted by the delight of holding her child for the first time but Dmitri wasn't so easily distracted.

'What's the problem?' he demanded in a low voice, leaning towards Katy to lessen the chance that Laurel would pay any attention. 'Tell me.'

He could see Lissa palpating Laurel's belly as

though…as though trying to tell by touch alone what was going on inside her, and he was suddenly struck by terror.

Was the placenta not separating properly? Was Laurel haemorrhaging—bleeding to death even as she was bonding with her son?

Before he could put his panic into words Lissa looked up at them with a wide grin of relief on her face.

'Why didn't anyone warn me that you were having twins?' she demanded, obviously relieved.

'Twins?' Dmitri gasped, and was even more shocked to hear Laurel echo the word in exactly the same way.

There wasn't time for any of them to question how Laurel could have been unaware of the fact she was carrying two babies, because the second one was already struggling to be born.

When Katy would have taken the first child from Laurel to allow her to concentrate on propelling the second one into the world, he beat her to it. He'd had years of practice at holding tiny babies but nothing felt the same as cradling this tiny boy safely against his heart. The fact that he was Laurel's child made him so very special.

When Laurel groaned with the renewed effort he was there to support her, murmuring soft words of encouragement in English and Russian when she swore that she didn't have the strength to continue.

Finally, the head was delivered, as dark-haired as its twin, but when the rest of the body slithered into view there was an important difference.

'*Dyevooshka!*' he announced proudly, this time

giving in to the urge to kiss the exhausted face now resting on his shoulder. 'Is a beautiful girl.'

In spite of the fact that they were two weeks early, the midwives seemed delighted with their healthy charges. It wasn't long before the second infant was wrapped in a blanket, too, and carried up to be introduced to her mother.

This time Laurel was too exhausted to do anything more than stroke the delicate skin of her daughter's cheek, so Dmitri sat close beside her, the very picture of a proud father, with a child cradled in each arm.

'Well, Daddy, what do you think of your babies?' Katy demanded with a broad smile, believing the answer was obvious.

Dmitri looked across the short distance that separated him from Laurel to meet her gaze.

'Daddy?' he murmured softly, knowing that only she would understand that he was asking a momentous question.

'Daddy,' she agreed with a tremulous smile, and he was so filled with a mixture of pride and anguish that he thought his heart would burst.

What had she done? Laurel thought the moment the word was out of her mouth.

Then she saw the delight in Dmitri's eyes as he gazed from one tiny being cradled so gently in his arms to the other, and knew she couldn't have lied.

No matter why it had happened or that their conception had been accidental or that she'd decided that he would probably have returned to Russia and forgotten about her long before she had a chance to tell him, she couldn't regret it. Not the babies or telling him that he was their father.

Oh, but she was so tired.

Too exhausted to cuddle both precious bundles when she couldn't even find the strength to raise a hand to touch Dmitri's sleeve.

Too exhausted to keep her eyes open even though she wanted to revel in the way Dmitri was placing a kiss on each dark head of hair with something that looked almost like reverence.

Straining to lift heavy lids, she could see that his lips were moving now, and guessed that he was probably talking to them. Knowing that he sometimes completely forgot his English in more emotional moments, she guessed that he was probably speaking Russian.

That would be good for them, to grow up bilingual, she thought, but was hazily aware that there was something wrong with the idea…

Something about the fact that she lived in England, thousands of miles away from his home, and that the babies wouldn't even be starting to talk before he disappeared out of their lives.

In the muddle of thoughts inside her head there was something about the fact that when their daddy left he would be breaking her heart, and she had a feeling that it would hurt just as badly as when she'd had to leave him.

There was something else… Something important that she wanted to ask him… Something about the possibility that, instead of going back to Russia straight away, he could…he could…what?

And then the thoughts ceased as sleep finally overtook her.

CHAPTER SEVEN

DMITRI took a last look at the frighteningly small bundles he'd just settled into their bassinets in the nursery before he left the room and closed the door behind him.

As he'd half expected, there was a reception committee waiting for him.

'Why didn't you tell us she was pregnant?' Lauren demanded, the sparks in her eyes almost enough to incinerate him.

He didn't dare smile, even though her straight-shooting methods amused him—so different from the almost mystic way she'd insisted that her unknown twin was trying to communicate with her. He was quite glad that she'd had to go back to her ward as soon as they'd returned to the hospital. At least it had spared him the third-degree until now.

'If we'd known she could be in labour, we could have called out the police, mountain rescue…oh, *dozens* of people to help us look for her,' she continued brusquely, still obviously tense.

'You saw how close she was to delivering,' she admonished him. 'She could have died in that car and we wouldn't have known until it was too late to do any…'

'Lauren, I didn't *know*,' Dmitri said fiercely, all amusement gone as he cut into her diatribe. 'You can count, so *you* do the maths. I haven't seen her for more than eight months and she said the babies are two weeks early. She wouldn't have known... *couldn't* have known that she was pregnant the last time I saw her.'

Nobody could have known that she was pregnant that night, because it was only then that those two precious beings had been conceived. But that was something just between Laurel and himself.

'So, how do you know they're yours?' Marc asked quietly, playing devil's advocate and voicing the disloyal question Dmitri had been asking himself right up to the moment he'd caught sight of them.

'Marc!' Lauren exclaimed. 'Are you implying that Laurel's the sort of person who'd—?'

'Whoa, sweetheart!' Marc said as he pressed a finger to her irate mouth. 'I'm not trying to impugn your sister's character, just establishing Dmitri's connection with your nephew and niece.'

Dmitri had no doubt that Marc had his hands full with Laurel's twin. Lauren certainly wasn't afraid to speak her mind or call him to account.

There was a serious point to Marc's question, but Dmitri had no doubts. He'd seen the photos Babushka Ana had treasured of his own childhood often enough to know that the pair sleeping in the room behind him were the product of *his* genes. For some reason his grandmother *still* treasured those pictures, in spite of the fact that her advancing Alzheimer's disease should have made them meaningless.

'Beyond the timing of their arrival and the fact that they resemble me as a child, there is one sure reason to be positive that they are my children—because Laurel told me so,' he said softly...forcefully.

These two had barely met her in the moments between rescuing her from her car and transporting her
to Denison Memorial. They didn't know her, but *he*
did, and for him her word was an absolute. 'I know,
now, that she may have been forced to do things she
didn't want to in the past, but she wouldn't lie about
something like that.'

Out of consideration for the patients sleeping in
nearby rooms he'd been careful to keep his voice
down, but he couldn't have made a bigger impact if
he'd shouted.

'Well,' said Lauren, already fiercely partisan about
her new relative, 'I'm glad you realise that.'

'Besides,' Dmitri added with a grin that was so
wide that it threatened to meet at the back of his head,
'you would only have to look at them and you would
know that I'm their father.'

'Can we?' Lauren demanded eagerly, as if she'd
been waiting for just such an opening. She clearly
wasn't in favour of hospital policy that only parents
could visit new babies in the first twenty-four hours.
'I promise not to disturb them.'

Dmitri couldn't resist the chance to have another
peep. He would have to sweet-talk his way past Lissa
if she caught him in the nursery again, but it would
be worth it.

With a finger to his lips he opened the door as
quietly as he could and led the way in on tiptoe.

There was one other baby in the room but, despite
the fact that it looked like a sleeping angel, none of
them spared it more than a glance.

'Oh, Dmitri, you were right,' Lauren breathed,
clearly fascinated as her eyes went from one tiny dark

head to the other. 'They look so much like you that it's ridiculous.'

'Thank you...I think,' he said with a grin. He didn't mind what anyone said, he was so proud of them that he hardly knew what he was doing or saying.

'When will they next wake up? I want to get my hands on them. Do you think Laurel would let me feed one while she feeds the other?'

He didn't stifle the chuckle quite swiftly enough. 'I think that could be a little difficult, unless there's something you haven't told me.' At her puzzled frown he elaborated. 'She's determined she's going to feed them herself, at least as long as she can produce enough milk to keep them happy.'

'Oh!' Lauren blushed, much to her husband's delight.

Dmitri was enchanted to see that the sisters shared the trait but doubted whether they would be equally pleased to learn of it. Laurel had always hated that he could bring colour to her cheeks so easily. Almost from the first time they'd met, all it had taken had been for him to step a little closer to her or an apparently innocent brush of his hand against hers.

'Dr Rostropovich!' hissed a voice behind them. 'What on earth are you doing in here again?'

'Oops! Caught!' he whispered to the other two, and turned to face the midwife standing in the doorway with her hands on her hips.

'Can't stay away, can you?' Lissa said in a scolding voice.

'Neither can you, obviously,' he countered cheerfully as he passed her, ushering Marc and Lauren out ahead of him. 'Admit it, you've fallen in love with my babies, too!'

'That's not the point. I'm allowed to be in here. Mr Fletcher, *you* put the security checks in place so you should know better. This isn't somewhere where visitors should be trooping in and out.'

'You're quite right, Lissa,' Marc replied as seriously as he could, while trying to keep his voice barely above a whisper. 'But in mitigation can I point out that the three of us *are* medically trained and could have been conducting a postnatal check on the babies?'

'No, you couldn't. None of you are paediatricians,' she said crisply. 'Now, go away until tomorrow morning. You know what time visiting hours start.'

All three of them were stifling chuckles like mischievous children as they turned away.

'Have you got somewhere to stay tonight?' Marc asked, as Lissa closed the door firmly behind them. 'You could stay with us, if you like. We'll be coming in first thing in the morning so we can bring you back with us then.'

'Thank you, but that won't be necessary. I already have a room at the hotel,' Dmitri said easily, not telling them that he had no intention of going there any time soon, even though it was so late.

As soon as Marc and Lauren left, he would be making his way to Laurel's bedside—not because he didn't trust the staff of Denison Memorial to take good care of her but because he *needed* to be there.

It wasn't something he had to think about, just a bone-deep certainty that he wouldn't be able to think about sleep until he'd reassured himself that, more by luck than judgement, Laurel was really here and not still part of a dream.

Now perhaps he'd have a chance to find out about the reasons that had forced her to leave him more than eight months ago.

He felt a brief resurgence of the mixture of disappointment and anger that had accompanied him on his search. It had been sheer determination to find out the answer once and for all that had prompted him to stay on in England rather than return immediately to Russia to spend some time with Babushka Ana.

His eyes roved over her sleeping form, so slender now that the babies had been born that she seemed scarcely more than a child herself.

He felt his lips tilt in a wry smile at the difference between his memories and the reality in front of him. He'd thought he'd known who Laurel was, having worked closely with her for nearly four months. He was only now realising just how complex a character she was, her beautiful face hiding secrets he'd never guessed.

Laurel drifted slowly and easily into wakefulness and somehow knew immediately that even *that* was different.

She slid a questing hand over the covers to confirm the fact that the birth of her babies hadn't been an all-too-real dream.

Twins!

Even the belated knowledge that *she* was one of a pair hadn't made her suspect that she was carrying two of her own. Perhaps, if she'd stayed in one place long enough for regular antenatal checks, a midwife would have realised that there were just too many heartbeats to go with all those limbs. As it was, they'd all had the most marvellous Christmas surprise.

Nikolai and Ana, she decided silently. They had been the names she'd decided on when she hadn't known whether she'd been expecting a girl or a boy, chosen to give them more than Russian blood as an inheritance.

They were beautiful babies, both with their father's dark hair. In time she would be able to see if they had also inherited his silvery grey eyes and the elegant planes and angles to their faces. It would be years before she knew whether they'd take after him in height, but she would be there for every millimetre of growth, loving and supporting in the way she'd always wished her own parents could have been.

That thought damped her euphoria, reminding her that, unlike today, she often felt as if she'd spent the whole of her life jerking to instant wakefulness and already filled with apprehension.

As a child it had been the knowledge that each day would probably be just like all the others that had gone before, a constant barrage of sniping that escalated every so often into outright demolition.

As an adult it had only grown worse, no matter how hard she'd tried to please, and the punishments and penalties had increased beyond belief.

It had taken her far too long, but at least she could be proud that she'd eventually found the inner strength to find a way to make a life for herself.

It had only been once she'd read that fateful letter that she'd been able to begin to understand what had driven Robert Wainwright to behave that way—understand, but never condone or forgive. It had also provided the important spur to try to break his hold once and for all.

Now she couldn't believe how naïve she'd been, to think that he'd just give up his plans when she fled his control to find her twin. It had been just days after she'd left that his bloodhounds had found her the first time, prompting her to run again.

That time, she'd taken the precaution of changing her name, dropping the first syllable to become Laurel Wright. That was the name under which she'd met Dmitri and she'd been granted a scant four months before she'd recognised the weaselly-looking man getting out of a hatefully familiar black car.

Her every instinct had been to grab her small cache of belongings and depart immediately, but she hadn't been able to do it. In that time she'd come to know Dmitri too well to leave without saying good-bye...hadn't been able to leave without seeing the man she'd fallen in love with just one more time.

She'd dreamed that they'd meet again one day. But she'd known even as she'd dreamed it that it was hopeless, never expecting it to happen. And yet, like a knight from the fairy stories she'd escaped into as a child, he'd found her and rescued her just when she'd needed him most.

Her decision to leave the motorway the way she had would have cost her and her babies their lives without Dmitri's perseverance, but it seemed as if she'd actually managed to evade the bloodhounds. At least she could be certain for a time that Robert Wainwright had no idea where she was.

Hopefully, that should give her a few days to recover from the birth and time to tell Lauren what had been going on. If Robert Wainwright discovered where she was, he would meet Lauren and find out that a twin existed. Then who knew what scheme he would hatch to get his way? She would have to warn Lauren as soon as possible to be on her guard. Tell her what Robert Wainwright was trying to do and why. And as for the babies...

A tide of remembrance washed over her, nearly drowning her in the memories of her terror-filled hours of labour.

If only she'd realised that she could have used the car horn to signal for help, perhaps she could have been rescued hours earlier and wouldn't have gone into premature labour.

How close she'd come to disaster.

If Dmitri hadn't stopped on precisely that stretch of road, and if he hadn't realised the significance of the sound he'd heard when she'd been trying to start her engine...

Dmitri.

Just thinking of him made her heart swell with a riot of emotions.

Joy to have seen him again when she'd believed that he was out of her life for ever.

Amazement that he should have been able to track her all the way up to Cumbria, let alone upside down in the middle of a snowy field.

Apprehension about what was going to happen, now that he knew he was the father of her children.

She must have made some sound in the early-morning silence of the room because suddenly a shadow moved against the curtains and resolved itself into the shape of a man.

'Laurel, are you all right?' Dmitri murmured anxiously as he stepped quickly to her side. 'Do you need something?'

'Dmitri,' she whispered with her heart in her throat as she gazed up at him. Her pulse was racing with the burst of adrenaline fired into her system when she'd thought him an intruder—the bloodhound, perhaps?

'W-what are you doing here?' she demanded breathlessly, that familiar melting sensation filling her at the sight of him, the way it had all those months ago.

'Didn't you know I would be here if you needed me?' he whispered back, and she heard the hint of reproach in his tone as well as his words.

He perched easily on the edge of the bed, the length of his leg seeming far too close to her for comfort, and the light filtering through the glass panel in the door from the corridor outlined his profile.

Her heart gave an extra thump when she remembered the last time she'd seen him lit like this. Not by torchlight at the scene of her accident but in his flat the night she'd come to tell him that she had to leave, that Robert Wainwright's investigators had located her again.

How could she have foreseen that he would just have finished a telephone call to Russia to speak to his Babushka Ana, or that he would be so heart-sick with worry over her that his need for comfort would be greater than her need to tell him she was going.

'Why did you go?' he demanded softly, almost as

if he had picked up on her thoughts. 'It couldn't have been because you were pregnant, because you didn't know...unless...' She saw a sudden look of horror cross his face. 'Unless you only came to me that night so I would...'

As ever, in moments of stress, his English deserted him, and there was a pause while he searched his mental dictionary to find an approximate translation.

'Did you only want me to mate with you so you could have babies?' he demanded stiltedly, and shocked her to the core.

'No, Dmitri! No!' she exclaimed, distressed that he could even think it. It had been the first time they'd slept together—the first time she'd ever made love. Had she been so inept and so distracted by the fact that it would be their only time together that she'd completely failed to show him just how much he meant to her?

'So?' he challenged. 'Why?'

She was so tempted to tell him that she'd begun to fall in love with him within minutes of their first meeting in the corridor; had been dreaming about the day they would declare their love for each other and share that ultimate intimacy. She wanted him to know that her heart had been breaking at the thought of leaving him, but there was a hardness in him that hadn't been there before so, at the last moment, she didn't dare lay her emotions bare.

'I didn't plan it, Dmitri. I swear it,' she said solemnly. 'I came to tell you that I would be leaving—to explain why—but when you opened the door and I realised how upset you were...'

She saw from the expression on his face that he

remembered his initial discomfort at being caught with the remnants of tears in his eyes. She would never know where she'd found the courage to step up close enough to put a consoling arm around his shoulders like that, and she'd been amazed that such a self-contained man had been willing to tell her of his pain.

The kiss he'd given her had been an innocent brush of his lips over hers, just an expression of gratitude for her concern, but it had been the match that had set off the conflagration and there had been no going back for either of them.

'So, why *did* you leave like that? In the middle of the night, without even saying goodbye,' he demanded.

'He had found me,' she said simply. 'He's been tracking me—or rather, his bloodhound has—ever since I left home to find Lauren, and I had to keep moving on. If I hadn't disappeared when I did, he would have taken me back to my...to Robert Wainwright.'

'He is your father, yes?'

'*No*,' she said emphatically. 'He is *not* my father. He's my uncle, but he adopted me when I was a baby.'

'And this was not a good thing?'

'Definitely not a good thing,' she agreed with feeling. 'I think he only did it so he could gain control of me—or rather, what I represented. It certainly wasn't because he wanted a daughter to love.'

'But you are *dvastat' vosyem*'—twenty-eight,' he pointed out with a painfully familiar frown. She'd seen those dark brows swoop together like that so often when he'd been worrying about one of their tiny

patients. 'You are old enough that he can do nothing
to stop you living your life now. Why is he a problem?'

'Because of what he wants me to do and the way
he's been trying to force me to do it,' she said, and
realised he wasn't following.

Before she could explain the family complications
that had brought the situation about there was a click
as the door was opened and a bassinet was wheeled
into view.

'Let's see if Mummy's awake and ready to see her
beautiful— Oh!' Lissa exclaimed, halting in both her
verbal and physical tracks when she saw her patient
had company.

'What are you doing here at this time of the morning?' she demanded crossly. 'And who let you into
the department? *I* certainly didn't.'

'No one let me in because I never left,' Dmitri
admitted softly, the fact that he'd made no attempt to
straighten up from his perch on the edge of her bed
tantamount to a challenge to the midwife's authority.

Laurel had to hide a smile at the look of outrage
on Lissa's face and then the resignation that followed
when she saw the resolution in his eyes. Obviously
she'd realised that he wasn't easily going to be
moved.

Laurel knew she should probably feel uncomfortable with the idea that Dmitri had been watching her
while she'd slept but she couldn't ignore the warmth
that spread through her at the thought that he'd been
watching over her.

'Well, you'll have to leave now,' Lissa said snippily, almost flouncing to the opposite side of Laurel's bed with the bassinet. 'It's time for the babies' feed.'

'As I'm here, I may as well make myself useful,' he countered. 'I can hold one baby while Laurel feeds the other.'

It was so eminently logical that it completely took the wind out of Lissa's sails for a moment. Then she regrouped.

'That depends on whether Laurel wants to have you here while she's doing something so...' She hesitated, but he didn't.

'So *intimate*?' he offered, his innocently questioning face completely at odds with the glance he sent towards Laurel. 'Is feeding a baby any more intimate than the process of making the babies in the first place?'

'Well, no, but...' Lissa floundered while Laurel fought a blush and tried to decide whether she *would* be too shy to feed the babies in front of him.

When she'd decided that her fear of appearing to be a totally inept novice in front of him was more embarrassing than the fact that he would be watching the process itself, she opted to rescue Lissa from an argument she could never win. For all that English wasn't his mother tongue, Dmitri had grown annoyingly adept at being able to tie people up in knots with his brand of logical debate.

'Lissa, I don't mind,' she said. 'Honestly,' she added when the flustered midwife still looked dubious. 'Just tell me which twin is most impatient and most likely to scream the hospital down, and I'll give him that one to pacify.'

Lissa chuckled at the wicked thought. 'It would

serve him right if you did,' she muttered as she lifted both babies with a well-practised scoop out of the bassinet they'd shared for the journey from nursery to ward. 'This little man has been raising the roof while his undercarriage was being dealt with. His sister is a patient little angel by comparison.'

Laurel found herself holding her breath as Lissa gently deposited her son in her arms.

'Hello, precious,' she whispered, and stroked a petal-soft cheek with a fingertip. Like a baby bird he turned towards her touch with his mouth open. 'Ah, single-minded, are you...?' She fumbled with the buttons at the neck of her nightdress.

'Here, let me help.' It was Dmitri, not Lissa, who was there to flick the buttons open, even as he cradled the second tiny bundle in the crook of his arm with practised ease.

Laurel's hands were trembling as she tried to work out the logistics of the process, but Dmitri made it seem as if it was an everyday occurrence to cradle his son's head in his hand while he showed her how to position herself comfortably.

'Thank goodness Nikolai doesn't need any instructions,' she muttered, feeling the heat of a blush radiating from her cheeks and wondering if it was ever going to recede. It had only been the slightest accidental brush of one knuckle across the curve of her breast but the contact had seared her right to the core. And *he* didn't even seem to have noticed that he'd touched her.

'Nikolai?' he questioned, an arrested expression on his face. 'You want to call him Nikolai? My second name?'

'If you don't mind,' she said shyly over the enthusiastic sounds of suckling. The baby in question obviously wasn't in the least bit self-conscious or interested in the momentous discussion going on around him. 'I thought I would call him Nikolai Dmitri.'

'And his sister?' his eyes didn't waver from hers, even to glance down at the child in his arms, their silvery grey gaze almost electric in its intensity.

'Ana Laura,' she said softly, joining the names of Dmitri's precious *Babushka* with the mother she'd never been able to claim until after her death, the mother she'd only come to know through that fateful letter.

This time when Laurel woke it was daylight.

Unlike the previous day when the ominous clouds full of snow had hung dark and heavy over the road ahead of her, today the sky was that clear icy blue so typical of winter days.

The reflection off the snow almost hurt her eyes as it poured into the room, making her peer around until she grew accustomed to the brightness.

It was several seconds before she realised that she wasn't alone in the room. Rather than leaving when she'd fallen asleep after feeding the babies, Dmitri must have appropriated the armchair in the corner beside the window and was now soundly asleep himself, despite his cramped position.

She smiled sadly at the memories it brought back— the way he'd been able to fall asleep in the most uncomfortable places and sleep as deeply as an exhausted child.

A sudden thought crossed her mind and she felt sick.

'Laurel?' Dmitri said, startling her. She hadn't realised that he'd woken while she'd been wandering through her memories.

'Are you all right?' he demanded. 'You're white like the...*snyek* outside. Shall I call Lissa?'

'No. I'm all right. It's just...' She shook her head.

'Please, there is *something* wrong. Tell me,' he said persuasively, adding proximity to his appeal as he settled himself on the edge of her bed again. 'If there is something I can do, you must tell me.'

'There's nothing you can do,' she said. 'I've been trying to deal with this problem for a long time now, and I just realised that I've made it worse.'

She felt her shoulders slump as she silently admitted what she was going to have to do.

There was only one thing really—disappear again, as quickly as possible, this time with two tiny babies in tow. She didn't really have a choice now that they'd been born.

Obviously, she couldn't leave immediately—she hadn't recovered enough from the delivery and the twins were still too young and too small to take them out of this protective environment.

She certainly couldn't leave them behind, not knowing how badly Robert Wainwright wanted her back under his control. If he got his hands on them, she wouldn't put it past him to try to use Nikolai and Ana as pawns to bargain with.

She shuddered at the thought of her precious children being subjected to the same sort of upbringing she'd had to endure.

No. Even living with one eye permanently over her shoulder would be better than that.

But, oh, it was going to be so hard to have to leave Dmitri again. She knew that this was just a brief visit on his part; he wasn't hers, could never be hers, but it had been nice, just for a few hours to enjoy having the man she'd given her heart to watching over her...

Suddenly suspicious of everyone's motives, she wondered if he'd had another reason for keeping such a close vigil over her. Instead of caring for her, had he been keeping an eye on her to make sure she didn't disappear before he got the answers he'd come for?

From those months when she'd been working with him, she knew how meticulous he was in his attention to detail. Was she just a loose end to be tied up before he finally went back to Russia for good?

'How many days do you think it'll be before I'm let out of here?' she demanded, then could have bitten her tongue off when she recognised the questions in his eyes. The last thing she needed if she was going to be able to slip away unnoticed was to raise his suspicions.

'You are in a hurry to go somewhere?' he asked, apparently casually, but she realised it was already too late. That analytical brain was now considering every possible reason why she might have asked the question.

'Nowhere special,' she said dismissively, which was perfectly true as far as it went. It wasn't *where* she was going that was important, just the fact that she kept moving often enough so that her uncle couldn't catch up with her.

Except...that wasn't really true any more, was it?

She'd spent all those months moving around while she was searching for Lauren. And now she'd found her, so she *didn't* need to move on. Once she'd had a chance to tell Lauren what was going on, she could actually confront the man and tell him he couldn't win.

The very thought of confronting him was frightening. But it was also quite...exciting, in a strange way, knowing that she now had some cards in her hand that he couldn't anticipate. Also, for the first time, it was likely that she would have some support from people who weren't dependent on Robert Wainwright for the roof over their heads or the wages in their pocket.

Was it possible that she might actually win this battle of wits and wills? She would have to wait until Lauren visited later on this morning, and as for Dmitri...

Suddenly Laurel was tired of keeping all her problems hidden. Long ago she'd trusted him with the story of her unwilling addiction to prescription drugs. Perhaps now was the right time to tell him the rest of the story. It might even help him to tie up all his loose ends so he could go back to Russia and Babushka Ana with a clear conscience.

The thought that he would soon be almost half a world away left her with an aching hollow where her heart should have been, but that loss was something she was going to have to deal with another day.

'Dmitri,' she began determinedly, 'there's something I haven't told you. It's about my family and the reason why I had to—'

She could have sworn out loud when there was a

sharp tap on the door, just when she'd gathered her courage, but she couldn't help smiling when she saw the bassinet appear in the opening, this time decorated with gaily bobbing balloons and pushed by a gloating Lauren.

CHAPTER EIGHT

'I SNEAKED in early,' Lauren announced with a beam, apparently oblivious to the fact that Laurel was staring at her as she gazed down at her charges.

Laurel suddenly realised that this was the first time she'd had a chance to look at her twin properly and she couldn't drag her eyes away, fascinated to see this person who resembled her so closely.

There was absolutely no doubt in her mind that they were identical, formed from the two halves of a single egg. She could just imagine the fun the two of them could have had with their classmates and teachers if they'd gone to the same school...but it had been fated not to be. Circumstances beyond their control had forced them to lose all those years together and there was no way they could be retrieved.

'There's another delivery in progress so no one had any objections when I offered to change nappies and wheel these two in to you. Now, do I get a hug for my reward?'

'Depends whether you're giving them or receiving them,' Marc warned as he followed her into the room, pretending to be jealous, then aimed a smile at Laurel. 'How are you feeling today?'

'A great deal lighter, thank you,' she joked with a telling glance down at her far-less-lumpy middle. 'I can actually turn over in bed without needing a crane any more. *And* I can see my knees again.'

'So, which one can I cuddle first?' Lauren demanded as she hovered impatiently over the bassinet.

There was a sudden bellow from one little body and they all laughed.

'That's obviously Nikolai,' Dmitri said a little smugly as he straightened up from the side of the bed to lift him out of the bassinet. 'He knows what he wants and when he wants it, and makes sure everyone knows about it.'

The bellow quietened to a half-hearted whimper as he carried the tiny bundle to Laurel's waiting arms.

Without batting an eyelid, he reached for the soft blanket that had been covering Nikolai in the bassinet and draped it casually over her shoulder to form a casual tent over the sleek dark head. It afforded her just enough privacy to spare her blushes at least until she felt a little more competent.

Not that Lauren and Marc seemed to be in the least bit interested in watching her feed her son. They were far more interested in cuddling Ana and bickering quietly over whose turn had gone on longer.

Both babies were fed, burped and were once more sleeping together in the bassinet when a sudden silence fell over the group.

Marc was the first to break it.

'Would you girls like the two of us to leave while you get to know each other?' he offered, totally ignoring Dmitri's scowl.

Laurel was bemused by his change of mood. Surely it didn't mean that he resented her new brother-in-law's suggestion. Perhaps it was because he didn't want to share their time together with anyone else, especially as he must be due to return to Russia soon.

'There must be some things that the two of you would find easier to talk about without an audience,' Marc continued considerately.

'Laurel?' Dmitri prompted, and she appreciated the fact that he'd given her the choice even though it apparently went against his own inclinations. Should she feel flattered that he didn't seem too keen to leave her side?

'Actually, if Lauren doesn't mind, I think I'd prefer to get the preliminaries over with while we're all here together. Then we won't have to keep repeating things.'

'That's fine with me,' Lauren confirmed with a smile for Marc. 'I don't think I've got any secrets left, at least not from Marc. Actually, he's been the one who was instrumental in discovering some things that I'd never known before—like the fact that I was one half of a set of twins.'

'Well, that's partly down to Robert Wainwright's interference, too,' Marc pointed out, and Laurel's blood ran cold.

'You *know* him?' she demanded in a shaky voice, wondering for one awful moment if the dreadful man had already ensnared Lauren and Marc into helping him with his evil scheme. Was she already too late?

'More than I ever wanted to,' Lauren said bluntly, then blushed. 'I'm sorry. That was very rude of me, considering he's your adopted father, but the wretched man kept insisting that *I* was Laurel Wainwright. He even set the police on me, insisting that I was an impostor pretending to be a ward sister and thereby endangering the health and safety of hospital patients. He made my life a misery for a while.'

'And mine,' Marc added, while he ruefully rubbed an elbow. 'Remind Lauren to tell you, some day, how she threw me over her shoulder in the car park because she thought I was one of his henchmen.'

Lauren pulled a contrite face at him but there was just enough laughter behind it for Laurel to feel a sharp stab of envy at their obvious happiness with each other.

She was so taken up with her thoughts, wishing that she and Dmitri could be looking forward to a lifetime of love together, that she almost missed the fact that Lauren was speaking again.

'Look, I'll apologise in advance if I'm speaking out of turn, but I got the feeling that Robert Wainwright isn't a very nice man...well, *obviously* he isn't or you wouldn't have taken off like that,' Lauren said, getting herself in a muddle as she contradicted herself halfway through.

'He is *not* a nice man.' Dmitri confirmed angrily, before Laurel could draw a breath. 'He has tried to control Laurel's life with drugs so she would do as he said, but she has been too determined for him.'

'But why would he want to do that? What's the point of drugging an adopted daughter... Oh, my God! He didn't try to...to abuse you, did he?' Lauren demanded in horror, one hand instinctively shielding Ana's head as though to protect her from the ugly subject of the conversation.

'No!' Laurel said at once. 'No. It was nothing like that. It was because of my *real* mother...I mean, *our* real mother, and her share of the company he manages.'

'This sounds like a long story,' Marc said as he

grabbed the chair flanking the bed opposite Laurel's in the four-bedded room. 'I'm going to make myself comfortable.'

Dmitri didn't have to move. He was once more happily ensconced on the edge of Laurel's bed, the powerful length of his thigh only separated from hers by the layer of bedclothes.

'Just a minute,' Lauren said impatiently...eagerly. 'You said our *real* mother. Does that mean you know who she is...*where* she is?'

Laurel wished her sister wasn't looking quite so excited. She didn't want to have to be the one to tell her that she was already too late to meet her.

But, then, if she hadn't died, Laurel would never have found out about Lauren's existence and known to come looking for her.

'I knew her as my aunt,' she began quietly. 'She was the sister of the woman who adopted me...Robert Wainwright's wife.'

At Lauren's insistence, she tried to give her a thumbnail description of the woman who had given birth to them, only to separate them immediately afterwards.

Lauren was downcast for a moment when she realised that she'd missed her chance of getting to know the woman, but brightened up to demand, 'I hope it won't come as too big a shock to know that I'm your *big* sister,' she said cheekily.

'Actually, once I knew you existed, I couldn't wait to meet you...to get to know you after all these years away from each other... And the fact that you were born first is one of the main reasons why I've been looking for you for more than a year,' she admitted.

She was already feeling lighter now that the moment had come. After today she would finally be free of the threat that had been hanging over her for so long—free to live her own life under her own terms.

'My fath— Robert Wainwright is far too greedy to let his plan fall apart without trying again,' she continued grimly. 'So I need to tell you just what he's trying to get one of us to do.'

Knowing that her explanation would be easier with the corroboration of the papers hidden inside her padded jacket, Laurel leant across to try to reach inside her bedside cabinet. She groaned as more than one set of muscles twinged in complaint.

Dmitri was there in an instant with a supporting hand and she had a fleeting wish that she was wearing something a little more alluring than one of the plain cotton tents she'd picked up on her travels.

'I can pass things to you, Laurel,' he offered gently. 'Tell me what you need.'

'My jacket, please. It's folded up in the bottom of my bag in the bottom of the cupboard.' She'd been so worried about letting it out of her sight before she'd had a chance to show Lauren the letter. If she'd had to wait to get the originals from the solicitor's safe-keeping it would have given Robert Wainwright extra time to put his plans into action, especially if his bloodhound had been hot on her trail on the way to Edenthwaite.

'Your jacket?' Lauren exclaimed, clearly concerned that she was going to try to leave. 'But you can't go. Not yet. What about the babies? They're too small to—'

'Hey!' Laurel chuckled. 'Don't panic! I only want

to get something out of it. Have you got a pair of scissors I can borrow for a minute?'

Mystified, Lauren handed over the pair from her uniform tunic pocket and Laurel saw her eyes widen when she began to unpick the lining of her jacket.

There was an almost breathless hush until she pulled out the envelope she'd concealed between the layers.

The silence was broken by Lauren's giggle.

'This is almost like one of those spy films, complete with the man with the Russian accent,' she pointed out, as Laurel slid the papers out of the slightly battered envelope and spread them on the bed.

The others joined in the laughter but Laurel was already concentrating on what she needed to explain.

'You'll have to forgive me if I get the chronology of the story a bit muddled, but I'll begin with this,' she said, holding up the photocopy of her mother's...*their* mother's letter.

'Obviously, these are all photocopies of the originals. I didn't dare bring those with me in case something happened to me, or to them. To make certain that Robert Wainwright couldn't use trickery to get hold of them, I arranged with our mother's old solicitor to hold them until I turn up in person.'

'Wise precaution,' Marc murmured. 'I wouldn't trust the man further than I could throw him, and I was only in the same room for a few minutes.'

Laurel threw him a wry look before she continued.

'Anyway, shortly after our mother died, this letter arrived at the house, addressed to me. It was just sheer chance that I saw it before Robert Wainwright did, or

I'm certain that I'd never have known of its existence.'

She handed the missive to Lauren and while she was reading it, gave the two men a brief résumé of its contents.

'That letter was the first time I found out who my real mother was. Until then, I'd always thought she was an aunt who preferred to keep herself rather distant from the rest of the family. It was also the first I knew of the fact that I'd been one of a set of twins.'

She held up copies of two birth certificates. 'She must have guessed that I'd have a hard time believing it because she enclosed these, to back up what she was saying. The letter also explains how she hadn't wanted to give us up but was forced into it against her will because of the scandal of our illegitimacy.'

'So why would that get Robert Wainwright in a lather?' Marc asked. 'He's a successful, wealthy businessman by all accounts. What difference would it make to him if the daughter he adopted all those years ago turns out to have an unexpected twin? Surely he wasn't worried that people would think he was a skinflint for being unwilling to take on both of you?'

'Hardly,' Laurel agreed.

'But the existence of a twin makes all the difference in the world if half of our family's company is going to belong to her,' his wife butted in with a militant look in her eyes.

Laurel knew she'd reached the bottom of the second page of the letter, apparently written not long before their mother's death, and she was smiling almost smugly as she reached for the other official document still lying on the bed and an article she'd printed from an internet search.

She'd hoped that Lauren would pick up on the significance of the spelling of their names in their mother's letter. All she had to do now was spell it out for the two men.

'Apparently, Robert Wainwright has been blustering around for years about ''his'' company, even though our mother was the real brains behind the scene. I don't know how long he'd been planning his little scheme, but once she died, he thought he'd be free to cash in on all her hard work and retire in luxury.'

'He was certain that all he needed to do was get Laurel to sign over her half of the company into his control. Then, as he already had control of his wife's half, he'd be free to sell it off to the highest bidder,' Lauren butted in, making Laurel feel rather slow-witted by comparison. It had taken her weeks to pull all the information together and Lauren had come to the same conclusions in a matter of minutes.

'Except the second half was our mother's half of the business and she'd put it in *Lauren*'s name, not mine,' Laurel continued, without missing a beat. 'She already knew that I was supposed to be inheriting my adoptive mother's half so when Lauren took up her inheritance, her two girls would own the whole company between us.'

'I suppose Wainwright just thought it was an unimportant typographical error?' Marc suggested. 'He must have thought that success was in his grasp.'

'Until Laurel disappeared without signing those crucial papers authorising his control over her mother's share of the business,' Dmitri said with what looked suspiciously like an expression of pride. 'And he's been chasing her all over the country while she tried to track you down.'

While he was speaking there was a commotion going on somewhere along the corridor. Both Marc and Lauren glanced towards the door, clearly loath to leave such an interesting meeting to find out what was happening.

The matter was settled for them when, without so much as a knock, the door was flung open unceremoniously and Robert Wainwright stormed in.

'Right, my girl. I've had just about enough of this nonsense,' he complained as he strode towards her, only slowing when he saw she wasn't alone. He paid absolutely no attention to the outraged midwife dogging his heels, trying fruitlessly to stop his entry.

Almost as if the manoeuvre had been rehearsed, all three of Laurel's visitors stepped closer to her, the men flanking her, one on either side, and Lauren standing protectively in front of the bassinet.

For the first time in her life, Laurel knew what it was like to have someone unequivocally on her side...three someones, she added silently while she fought the sudden heated prickle of tears.

The lean hand that covered hers, the strong fingers threading securely between her own slightly shaky ones gave her self-esteem a much-needed boost.

She glanced quickly up at Dmitri, knowing that she would meet those liquid silver eyes. She was startled to find them full of belief and admiration until she remembered that he was the one person in the room who knew just how many obstacles she'd had to overcome to get to where she was today.

That was enough to banish the tremors and she straightened her shoulders and lifted her chin ready for battle.

The poor midwife was still hovering in the doorway, not quite knowing what to do for the best. Laurel met her worried gaze and sent her a reassuring smile to let her know everything was under control. She looked very relieved when she silently let herself out of the room, but Laurel was certain she would be hovering somewhere not too far away in case reinforcements were needed.

Meanwhile, Wainwright's glower had been sliding from one of her companions to the other as if they were totally unimportant, then he deliberately focused the full force of his ire on her.

She actually saw the moment of disbelief when he realised that she wasn't going to cower any more, but that didn't stop him from trying to bluster his way to what he wanted.

'I understand you've inherited your mother's morals,' he sneered with a dismissive glance towards her precious babies. 'Well, I won't spoil your little party—just interrupt it long enough to complete some family business, if your friends will give us some privacy.'

'Oh, I don't mind my friends knowing what's going on,' Laurel said cheerfully, deliberately ignoring the slur on her mother's name for the moment. 'What exactly *is* this family business that had you sending bloodhounds after me all over the country? It must have been very important if it brought you all the way up to Edenthwaite in a snowstorm.'

She didn't think anything could feel better than finally standing up to the man, then Dmitri squeezed her hand and there was that special gleam in those liquid silver eyes and she knew she was wrong. It seemed that anything she did felt better if this man was beside her when it happened.

'Don't you try to act clever with me, my girl,' he growled as he dragged a sheaf of papers out of the inside pocket of his expensive-looking overcoat. 'You know I need your signature on these business papers, so just do as you're told.'

Silently, Laurel held out her free hand, almost spoiling the drama of the scene with a chuckle when she realised how imperious she must look—almost like a queen on her throne surrounded by her courtiers.

With a snort of impatience he stepped just close enough to hand the papers over, rightfully wary of getting too close to a visibly bristling Dmitri.

After the briefest of perusals—just long enough to see that her suspicions had been correct—Laurel dropped the papers dismissively onto her lap.

'I'm sorry, but I couldn't possibly sign these,' she said politely.

'What the...? Why not?' he demanded, then his eyes narrowed suspiciously. 'It's money, isn't it? Well, if you think you can blackmail me into giving you any—'

'Oh, no,' she interrupted icily. 'Money hasn't got anything to do with it. Apart from the fact that I'm perfectly capable of earning my own living without expecting handouts, I couldn't sign the papers because it would be illegal.'

'What do you mean, *illegal*?' he snapped, using almost the same impatient tone with her as he had when she'd been five. 'It's a common or garden document that allows me to act as your proxy in dealings for the company, now that you've inherited part of it.'

'That's why it would be illegal,' she said patiently, suddenly realising that after feeling so helpless for all those years, she was actually enjoying every minute of stringing the objectionable man along. 'I can't sign because the share of the company to which those documents refer isn't mine, it's my sister's.'

'Rubbish!' he scoffed. 'You don't know what you're talking about. Your brain's probably too scrambled by all those tablets you have to take.'

Laurel couldn't help the sound of triumph creeping into her laughter, but there was an undercurrent of bitterness, too.

'I hate to tell you this, Uncle Robert,' she said, determined that she would never call him her father again, 'but I haven't taken anything stronger than an aspirin for a headache since before I started my nursing training.'

There was a special triumph in telling him *that*, one that Dmitri's tightened grasp told her he endorsed to the full.

As for the sight of the man who had frightened and disappointed her all her life now standing there with his face purple and his mouth open, that was a detail that she would have to enjoy later.

'And my brain is certainly clear enough to understand the significance of our mother leaving her half-share of the company to Lauren. It meant that she knew what you were going to try to do and was putting it out of your reach. As for the other half, it's up to my adoptive mother if she decides to leave you in charge of it. My only concern,' she continued, bulldozing over his belated attempt to interrupt, 'is that if you get overall control of the company, you'll sell it to that conglomerate mentioned in the papers just to line your own pockets. Then the people who have worked for the company for so many years would just end up on the scrap heap, thrown out by a notorious asset stripper even more greedy for profit than you are.'

'And as *I'm* the Lauren mentioned in our mother's will,' Lauren declared, taking the floor without a hitch, almost as if the two of them had planned it that way, 'I will be the new owner of the relevant half-share of the company, once the proper papers have been signed. In the meantime, you have no authority to make any take-over or merger deals, so you needn't waste any more of your time up here in Edenthwaite because *I* won't be signing your papers either.'

'In fact, Laurel,' Marc added with more than a touch of malice in his conversational tone, 'I think it would be a very good idea if we let that nice policeman who investigated Mr Wainwright's harassment have a look at those papers, just to ascertain whether there are grounds for criminal proceedings.'

'And the police should also investigate the drugs he forced Laurel to take for many years,' Dmitri chimed in grimly. 'This is definitely something illegal.'

Laurel saw the way Robert Wainwright's eyes went frantically from one to the other of them and finally fell on the incriminating papers resting on her lap.

For a moment she wondered whether he was actually going to have the cheek to try to grab them from her, then saw him bare his teeth like a cornered rat when he recognised the futility of trying.

'You're welcome to the damn company,' he snarled. 'I don't need it any more.' And he stormed back out of the room as precipitately as he'd come in.

'Hmm,' Marc said, a welcome peace descending over the room after the swirling emotions of the last half-hour. 'That was an interesting parting shot.'

'What do you mean?' Lauren asked.

'I mean that I think it would be a very good idea if I phoned the police sooner rather than later. I wouldn't be at all surprised to find that he's been skimming money out of the company for years.'

'You think he will go with this money?' Dmitri enquired sharply.

'I think he had every intention of disappearing to somewhere without an extradition treaty sooner or later, but he was greedy enough to want to have it all—hence the final throw at the merger.'

'You've still got that policeman's number in your office, haven't you?' Lauren prompted.

'Yes, and there's no time like the present,' Marc said with a malicious smile. 'We wouldn't like to let our dear departed friend get too far before he's picked up. The last thing we want is to have to hunt for him all over the country.'

The two of them hurried out, Lauren pausing just long enough to fawn over the babies one last time.

Laurel drew in a deep breath and blew it out in a steady stream, needing to calm herself down after the heady experiences of the recent encounter.

'Oh, Dmitri!' she exclaimed, almost bouncing up and down in the bed as excitement bubbled over again in spite of her best efforts. 'I can hardly believe it's over at last. Do you realise what that means? I can live my own life—I don't have to move on. I can stay here as long as I like and get to know my sister.'

It was several very long seconds before he answered, and she was quite disappointed by his lack of response.

Had she misread the situation? He'd spent a long time searching for her and had stayed by her side long after the babies had been born. And he'd been so protective when her uncle had tried to bully her that she'd actually thought she meant something special to him.

The stony expression he wore now told a different story.

'It is good to know that you will have what you want at last,' he said quietly, as he released her hand and straightened up to stand beside her bed, his expression strangely sombre and his accent oddly clipped.

It hardly seemed like the same curiously liquid pronunciation that had captured her imagination the first time he'd spoken to her in that hospital corridor.

His eyes had changed, too, the lively sparkle completely missing from them and leaving her feeling almost as bereft as the loss of their physical contact.

'I am glad you have found your family at last,' he added, sounding quite formal and almost impersonal, and she felt suddenly close to tears.

This reaction wasn't what she'd expected at all.

She'd thought he'd be pleased for her that Robert Wainwright's influence was no longer going to be affecting her every action.

All the time the man had been in the room, trying to intimidate her, Dmitri had stayed supportively close to her with his hand meshed tightly with hers in case she needed to borrow his strength.

Unfortunately, it seemed as if, almost as soon as her uncle was gone, so was the support.

Laurel had the horrible feeling that something she needed in her life almost as much as breathing was slipping away through her fingers, and she had no idea how to stop it.

Or was she just overwrought after her showdown with Robert Wainwright?

'What did you think of my sister? And Marc?' she asked, grabbing desperately for a topic that would prove that the Dmitri she knew was still in the room with her. She wasn't very comfortable with this stranger.

'I like them. Both of them,' he said with a brief smile. 'When I told them that you must be lost, they straight away wanted to search. If we had not found you, they would still be searching, too.'

He glanced down at his watch and she realised with a pang that he was going to leave.

Over the last few hours she'd grown accustomed to the fact that he seemed to want to be with her. It had been all too easy to get comfortable with the idea that he was a permanent presence in her life.

She'd known from the first day she'd met him, a year ago, that he'd been due to return to Russia at some stage. But that had been before he'd found out about Nikolai and Ana. Wasn't their existence enough to make him change his plans; to stay with her?

She'd had no option but to walk away from him all those months ago, and she'd wondered for eight long months if the pain of losing him would ever ease. She didn't know how she'd survive if he were to leave the room now, and she never saw him again.

'If you will excuse me, I must try to find a telephone. Then I need to fetch my car.'

'But you will be coming back?' she demanded before she could curb her tongue, hating how pleading she sounded.

She'd managed to survive on her own when she hadn't dared to trust anyone, but it was different with Dmitri. She didn't *want* to be without him, not now that she'd seen him again. Not now that she'd seen the love in his eyes when he held their babies.

'I'll be back,' he said quietly, but didn't seem in the least bit happy at the prospect.

CHAPTER NINE

DMITRI strode away from Laurel's room with only one thought in his head. He wanted to hit something...hard.

'*Gwoopahst!*' he hissed as he made his way towards Marc's office. 'Stupidity!' he repeated in English, just for good measure, then wondered why he bothered. He wasn't going to need much of his hard-won English once he was back in Russia.

He tapped briskly on the door then entered at Marc's invitation.

'Dmitri. Take a seat,' the hospital administrator invited easily, coming out from behind his desk to perch one hip on the corner of the paper-strewn surface. 'Lauren has just gone up to her ward again, but I can tell you that you've put me in a difficult position.'

'*I* have?' Dmitri blinked, glad that there was a smile behind the unexpected accusation. He didn't accept the offer of a seat because he was still too wound up to be able to sit still, far too many thoughts chasing each other round inside his head.

'Of course, because now that she's seen *your* two, Lauren is expecting *me* to be able to give her twins, too. Talk about performance anxiety!'

Dmitri found it difficult to join his laughter, especially when he knew his time with those precious babies was limited to days, or even hours.

Laurel's words were still echoing in his ears, and with them the death of his fledgling dreams.

It's over at last… I can stay here and get to know my sister, she'd said, and he'd suddenly realised how selfish he was being. Why on earth had he thought that she would be willing to move halfway around the world just so that he could have her and their babies with him?

And it *was* that order of importance, he'd realised with a shock.

It didn't seem to matter that he was devoting his working life to saving and caring for newborn babies, or that Nikolai and Ana could have died if Laurel hadn't been found in time.

His love for his children had been instantaneous and total and he would fight to the death if anyone threatened them, but it was *Laurel* who mattered above all, Laurel he loved more than his next breath.

He desperately needed to talk to someone, but the one confidant he'd had for so many years was no longer able to understand what he was talking about most of the time, let alone able to give advice.

Marc picked up on his sombre preoccupation straight away.

'Is there a problem—something I can do for you?' he offered quietly, and Dmitri was grateful for his perception.

'Would it be possible for me to make a long-distance phone call? I can write you a cheque for the cost of the call.'

'No problem,' Marc said immediately. 'Is that long-distance within this country, or a call to Russia? Do you need a directory?'

'To Russia,' he confirmed as the ache intensified around his heart. 'And I have the number, thank you.'

With a gesture towards one of the phones on his desk, Marc tactfully slipped out of the room and Dmitri tapped out the familiar numbers.

This should have been such a joyous call to make, letting Babushka Ana know that she'd just been made a great-grandmother. Instead, he would probably end up trying to talk to a woman who no longer remembered who he was, to tell her about babies he was going to have to leave behind.

Even when the voice at the other end of the line told him that his grandmother was having an unexpectedly good day, it didn't prepare him for the cheerful voice that greeted him when his only relative was brought to the phone.

Five minutes later, when there was a gentle tap on the door, he was still sitting behind the desk with tears of disbelief trickling down his cheeks.

'Dmitri? Did you get through?' Marc asked as he carried in two steaming cups, then caught sight of his face. 'Good Lord. Are you all right? What happened? Was it bad news?'

'Not bad news. Good news,' Dmitri said, suddenly realising that his cheeks were wet and fumbling in his pocket for a handkerchief. 'The *best* news,' he corrected himself as he leapt out of the chair, only realising at the last moment that Marc would probably be horrified if he were to give him a bear hug in celebration.

'So, was it something about your next post? Did you get the position you wanted?' He handed Dmitri one of the cups and set the other one down on his desk. 'I'm still waiting to find out about a new medical post. I can't wait to escape from this room and get back into *real* medicine again.'

Dmitri wasn't in the mood to be sidetracked into general conversation, not when he needed to tell someone...

'I phoned Babushka Ana—my grandmother—to let her know about Nikolai and Ana.'

'I expect she was delighted, especially that you named your daughter after her.'

'Marc, she has Alzheimer's disease,' he explained, hating the very sound of the word for what it had done to such a loving woman. 'She has been thinking I am her son for months now instead of her grandson. But today...'

'Oh, damn, Dmitri. That must be rough,' Marc sympathised. 'Especially when you're so far away from her.'

'I am thousands of miles away, but most days she is even further,' he said, feeling the press of tears again. 'Then today they give her the telephone and suddenly she is speaking to me like we are in the same room before the disease got so bad. And when I tell her about the babies and their names and that they look just like the photographs she has in her room—the photographs of me when *I* was a child— she *thanked* me.'

He had to pause to swallow the emotions that threatened to overwhelm him all over again.

'She thanked me for letting her know that our family had a future,' he whispered brokenly, still not quite believing that it had happened.

He would never know what miracle it was that had

allowed her increasingly damaged brain circuits to fire well enough on this particular day. All he knew was that the miracle had allowed her to understand what he was telling her and had allowed her to express her joy at his news.

After all these weeks and months of trying to hold a long-distance conversation with a stranger, for just a little while it had been almost like having her back the way she used to be.

He knew it was unlikely to happen again—it shouldn't logically have been possible this time—but in a way her return to dementia would make things easier for him when he went to visit her on his return to Russia.

'She will have forgotten all about it by the time I see her,' he continued sadly, hoping his voice didn't sound as rough as it felt. 'Both the conversation and the fact that there is a tiny person with her name so far away.'

At least, when he saw her, he wouldn't have to speak about the precious babies he'd had to leave behind, or about their mother, who would be staying to get to know the twin she'd just met for the first time.

And it didn't help the ache in his heart to know that even if Laurel had wanted him to stay with her and her precious babies, it wouldn't be possible.

'You don't have to go yet, do you?' Marc demanded, clearly surprised. 'Surely you could delay for a few more weeks...months even, while the babies are so small?'

Dmitri wouldn't even allow himself to daydream that scenario. It would hurt too much.

'Babushka Ana probably won't recognise me the next time I visit her, but that is no reason to abandon her,' he said firmly. 'At least *I* know that I am there for her when she has no one else, the way *she* was there for me when I was all alone in the world.'

And it was love, not duty or guilt, that had him phoning every week while he was so far away, and visiting every week when he was close enough.

'Anyway, I have a responsibility to the Russian hospital that enabled me to spend this year in the English neonatal unit,' he said simply. 'The least I can do to repay is to pass on what I have learned to my colleagues.'

'The trouble is, life is never just black and white,' Marc said cryptically. 'There is duty and honour and responsibility, which are all so basic that they are easy to follow, but if your heart becomes involved, suddenly nothing is simple any more.'

Dmitri smiled at Marc's philosophical mood, but couldn't agree with his conclusions. *Everything* was very simple, as far as he could see, whether hearts were involved or not.

In Russia, he had a grandmother he loved who had loved him all is life, and a job to which he owed his loyalty; here, he had a woman he loved and the children they'd created together. If it were just *his* choice whether he stayed here or returned to Russia, it would tear him in half because his heart couldn't be in two places at once. And to think he'd once believed that it would break his heart when he had to leave his precious sports car behind.

Even the logical alternative was impossible—for Laurel and the babies to go to Russia with him—

because he cared more about Laurel's feelings than about his own.

If she hadn't just been reunited with her twin and, more importantly, if she'd ever told him she loved him, then he would have dared to ask her to come with him. But that was just crying after the moon.

Not only had she never said the words, but the fact that Laurel hadn't even cared enough about him to tell him she was leaving him—not even when they'd just been together in his bed—well, that told him how important he was to her.

And he had too much Russian pride to set himself up for outright rejection again.

'So, when will you be leaving?' Marc asked, reading between the lines all too accurately. 'Can you stay until Laurel's ready to leave hospital? Lauren's thinking of inviting her and the babies to stay with us until she decides where she wants to live.'

Laurel leant back against the pile of pillows, holding Ana up to her shoulder.

She was supposedly bringing up her daughter's wind, but her eyes were fixed on what was happening at the other end of the bed.

Dmitri was sitting there again, the way he had been at every feed time, this time with a rather fussy Nikolai cradled in his arms.

There was just something about the sight of a big man holding a tiny baby with such gentleness and competence that completely melted her heart. She'd thought so the first time she'd seen Dmitri holding one of their tiny charges when they'd worked together, and now that the child was their own, the effect was stronger than ever.

But, then, everything the man did had that effect on her, from the wicked grin he used to throw her way every time he saw her to the way his eyebrows drew into a dark V when he was concentrating. And the effect of his touch...

No. She wasn't going to think about that, not when he was sitting just feet away from her, almost close enough to touch. She didn't *dare* think about how good they'd been together, not with the way he'd been behaving towards her over the last twenty-four hours. If she did, she'd probably cry.

He'd promised to return after he'd collected his precious car, and he had, but somehow he seemed to have turned into a complete stranger. If she didn't know better, she might almost think that *he* was the one with a twin, someone who barely looked in her direction and certainly didn't send her wicked grins.

And it was all so frustrating because she had the strange feeling that it was all somehow *her* fault that he was behaving like this.

Well, if she didn't ask, she'd never find out, and she certainly couldn't stand another minute of this sticky atmosphere between them.

'Dmitri, have I said something to upset—?' she'd begun, when there was a sudden tap at the door and Lissa stuck her head round.

'Dmitri, could I have a word?' she asked hurriedly, obviously a refugee from the delivery room with her mask drooping around her neck.

'Sure,' he said, beckoning her in.

'Actually,' she began hesitantly, only stepping into

the room far enough for the door to swing closed, 'we've got a problem in the delivery room and I wondered if you'd be willing to have a look?'

'A problem with a baby?' he demanded, his gaze instantly razor sharp. 'How many weeks gestation? Has it arrived already or is the mother still in labour?'

It seemed to Laurel that he'd positioned Nikolai in the bassinet almost without realising he was doing it, the questions coming thick and fast.

'He's full term, already arrived and he's got a severe cleft palate, but it's his colour and breathing I'm not happy about...' Lissa was explaining as he strode towards her, and that was the last Laurel heard for some while.

It wasn't until her meal arrived a couple of hours later that she caught up on the gossip.

'Apparently the word is all over the hospital,' said the orderly who delivered the tray. 'Your young man took one look at that poor little baby and told them to get ready to send it straight to the city hospital in an ambulance.'

Laurel's eyes widened. What problems had Dmitri found that had needed immediate referral? It must have been something life-threatening and something that he was pretty certain that Denison Memorial couldn't handle.

'Does the gossip say what was wrong?' she prompted, knowing she would have to take the information with a pinch of salt as such tales always grew out of all proportion.

'Well, I didn't see him, but someone said his little face was a mess, poor beggar—it'll take more than one operation to put *that* right—but they said his heart had been plumbed in wrong and his brain was going to die if it wasn't put right, sharpish.'

Laurel squashed the urge to smile at the terminology. If the woman was right and the main blood supply to and from the heart had developed in the wrong positions, the poor child did have some serious problems.

She didn't envy Lissa her luck. What were the chances of having two 'problem' deliveries in as many days?

First there had been her unexpected twins, and now a cardiac anomaly, both of which should have been picked up on ultrasound scans to avoid last-minute complications.

It couldn't be good for this latest baby to have to travel any distance with his heart unable to do the job it was intended to do. If his condition had been diagnosed, he could have been born in a facility that was prepared to deal with his problems as soon as he arrived.

'Not hungry?' Lauren asked as she came in with her arms full of parcels and pushed the untouched tray aside. 'Denison's food is better than most, but it's still ''institutional'' cooking. If I promise to do better than this, would you be willing to chance staying with Marc and me when you're ready for discharge?'

'That's very kind of you but—'

'You don't have to give me an answer now. Think about it. In the meantime, how about opening some of these? I had *such* a good time shopping.'

Laurel was overwhelmed and tried to tell her that she shouldn't have been so extravagant, but Lauren wasn't listening.

'Start with this one,' she demanded, pushing a flat, floppy parcel adorned with a silky bow at her. 'I'm a firm believer that the babies shouldn't get all the presents. Mother's need some pampering, too.' She gave a cheeky grin. 'That's a strong hint, so make sure you remember it when it's my turn,' she said.

Laurel started to peel the flaps back but Lauren was far too impatient.

'Not like that! It takes too long!' she exclaimed as she grabbed hold of one edge of the paper and ripped it back. 'What do you think? Isn't it gorgeous?'

It was the sort of glamorous nightdress that Laurel had only dreamed about, all shimmering silk and lace and so cleverly made that it didn't look in the least as if it had been designed to make feeding a baby easier.

'Gorgeous,' she agreed, almost speechless at the generosity of the gift.

'Another thing for you to remember,' Lauren teased. 'Now open the rest.'

There were tiny stretchy sleepsuits in pink and blue and thickly padded 'snowsuits' ready for their first venture out into the big wide world, and two teddy bears that were bigger than their recipients.

'Crazy, aren't they? I know they're too big to fit in their bassinets but they were so soft and huggable— and washable—that I just couldn't resist.'

'And that's another thing I've got to remember for later, I suppose,' Laurel said with a grin as they cuddled one each.

They fell quiet then, but it wasn't an uncomfortable silence. In fact, it almost felt as if they were old friends getting together after a lengthy absence, both with much to tell of the things they'd done since they'd last seen each other.

'I always felt…'

'I always knew…' they began together then stopped with a chuckle.

'You can go first, as you're the baby,' Lauren offered.

'No. Age before beauty,' Laurel countered wickedly. 'If you're going to hold those few minutes over me for the rest of our lives, I'm going to start retaliating.'

They both seemed to realise at the same moment how much that had sounded like sibling bickering because they both laughed.

'Oh, Lord, is this what I've got to look forward to with Nikolai and Ana?' Laurel asked plaintively. 'Are they going to fight like cat and dog?'

'Probably,' Lauren said disgustingly cheerfully. 'And if I have twins, too…'

'Bite your tongue, woman! In fact, don't even think about it,' Marc ordered in apparently horrified accents as he joined them. 'I'm hoping that having Laurel and her two come to stay with us will put you right off the idea altogether.'

'No chance,' Lauren said as she snuggled up to him and cast longing glances towards the bassinet. Nikolai had been slightly restless for some time but didn't seem to want to oblige her by waking up for a cuddle. 'I'm really looking forward to the prospect of bringing both our families up in one big happy muddle.'

Laurel didn't know what drew her gaze across to the door at that moment, other than the fact that she'd always been somehow more aware of Dmitri's pres-

ence than any other man's. What she hadn't expected
to see was the look of pain that etched his face as he
watched the three of them laughing and joking together.

She longed to hold her hand out to him to invite
him into the circle, hoping that would banish whatever thought was hurting him, but in the next moment
the expression was wiped off his face as though it
had never existed.

For the next few minutes he was plied with questions about the little boy he'd volunteered to accompany on his journey in the ambulance.

Laurel was as glad as any of them that he'd seemed
to be determined to maintain his hold on life, and that
he would soon have the surgery to correct the func-
tion of his heart.

Her pleasure that it looked as if the baby would
survive was tempered by the wish that Lauren and
Marc would decide it was time to go home. She
needed privacy to speak to Dmitri, to see if she could
find out what had put that unhappy expression on his
face, but that was unlikely all the time Lauren thought
she might get her hands on one of the twins.

As if he'd read her thoughts, Nikolai let out a wail
and with a cursory 'May I?' Lauren scooped him up
into her arms.

For a couple of moments she cooed at him, hoping
he'd quieten long enough for her to have a cuddle,
but he wasn't to be placated.

'Here you are, Mum, one starving baby wanting
food,' she said as she handed him over.

Laurel smiled, but inside she'd started to feel increasingly insecure, frightened that she was going to fail her babies.

In spite of the unexpected arrival of twins, she'd really hoped that she was going to be able to feed them herself. She knew it would take several days before her milk supply would build up, but Katy, the other midwife who had been present at their birth, had told her earlier that they'd had to supplement Nikolai's feed with a small bottle of formula during the night.

Now she was having to face the possibility that she would have to give them formula as well as, if not instead of, her own milk.

'Are you a hungry boy?' she murmured as she settled him in the crook of her arm. Before she could undo the first button on her bodice Dmitri was there to drape a white cotton blanket over her shoulder to shield her exposed breast. 'Thank you,' she whispered, wanting so much to say more but hardly daring to meet his eyes for fear she would weep.

This was the Dmitri she'd known and loved when they'd worked together, talked together, laughed together. This was the gentle considerate man who had been her first and only lover, the father of the children he obviously adored every bit as much as she did.

So why was he distancing himself from her?

Was it still because of the way she'd left him before? She'd thought he understood why she'd had to go, especially as he now knew what Robert Wainwright was like.

Was it resentment over the fact that she hadn't told him about her pregnancy, or could it just be that he was preoccupied, perhaps with something to do with his grandmother?

She forced herself to take a steadying breath as she reached for the bottle of formula, hoping that Nikolai was full enough not to want it this time. It wouldn't do her any good if she let herself get all worked up— in fact, it might even slow the build up of her milk supply.

Her heart fell when Nikolai latched onto the plastic nipple and began to swallow greedily. It almost seemed as if she had produced less this time than last if his eagerness was anything to go by.

In which case, it was imperative to speak to Dmitri as soon as possible. She didn't want anything to interfere with the health of her precious babies, especially if it was something that could be solved with a few questions and answers.

At least it should be fairly easy to find the right time to have such an important conversation. With Dmitri spending so much time with the babies, it was just a matter of waiting for her other visitors to leave.

'So, Laurel, are you going to be coming to us when you and your babies are ready to leave Denison?' Marc asked over the top of Lauren's head as she cuddled Ana. 'I was going to suggest that Dmitri join us but he's expecting to be going back to Russia any day now.'

CHAPTER TEN

LAUREL found herself staring at the snowflake cut-outs that someone had stuck to the window in preparation for the rapidly approaching Christmas season, without really being able to focus on them.

There was a roaring sound in her ears and it must have been sheer maternal instinct that had prevented her from dropping her tiny son when the shock had hit her.

Dmitri was going back to Russia *soon*? And he hadn't said anything to her?

· Well, that certainly told her just how unimportant she was in his eyes. Even Marc had known and he'd only met the man a couple of days ago.

She felt almost as if the rest of the world had ceased to exist for a moment as she concentrated on taking her next breath. But they were there, and she knew it, even if she didn't dare to look to see if they were aware of her shock and guessed at the reason for it.

She put the half-empty bottle down and went to lift Nikolai up to her shoulder to help him bring up his wind when, without any warning, he opened his mouth and projected his entire meal across the bed and onto the floor.

'Ay! *Astarozhna!*' Dmitri exclaimed, narrowly escaping the flood as he hurried to help her. 'Was it wind that did this?'

'I don't think so,' Laurel said, her hands shaking as she tried to support Nikolai with one and undo his sodden clothing with the other.

Coming on top of her shock at hearing of Dmitri's imminent departure, this was something she didn't need, she thought as she peeled his little sleepsuit off.

'He's got a rash!' she exclaimed when she got her first look at his naked body. 'And he feels hot...very hot. Dmitri, what's the matter with him? He's been restless all morning.'

She couldn't believe that she'd automatically turned to him in her panic, not when he was about to desert them without a word. Then, in the blink of an eye, she saw Dmitri's professional instincts come into play as he began to examine the little body now shaking with outraged wails, and knew she would never trust anyone else with her child in the same way.

It wasn't until she saw him reach for the empty water glass on the bedside cabinet and watched him press it over some of the spots that she realised what he was looking for.

'Is it meningitis?' she gasped, terrified. 'It can't be. He's not even two days old.' She was sure she remembered that the case they'd had in the neonatal unit all those months ago had been five days old. But what really terrified her was the memory that the poor child's brain had been irreparably damaged by the bacteria.

'Is *not* meningitis,' he said firmly. 'Look, Laurel, when I press the spots they disappear.'

'Then what *is* it?' she cried helplessly, wanting to wrap Nikolai tightly in her arms but knowing that she had to allow Dmitri to continue his examination.

Laurel wasn't sure what she was pleading for when she looked up into his face—answers, reassurance or just the comfort of knowing that someone else cared as much as she did. When she saw that underneath his calm medical persona he was feeling exactly the same fear that she was, she realised that the soul-deep sense of connection that had been between them when this sick child had been conceived was still there.

'Well, it's too soon for symptoms of pyloric stenosis,' he said, dragging his eyes away from hers to concentrate on the little body lying across her lap. 'That's usually about four weeks after delivery and wouldn't explain the rash.'

'It couldn't just be something as simple as heat rash, could it?' Lauren suggested, and Laurel blinked. She'd almost completely forgotten that her twin was standing there with Ana in her arms.

'I don't think so.' Dmitri shook his head. 'That's usually accompanied by dehydration, not projectile vomiting, and the rash is different.'

'But Ana's all right, isn't she?' Laurel asked fearfully. 'If they've been together and it's some sort of infection...' She paused, waiting while Marc helped Lauren to open the tiny sleepsuit. When they exposed her daughter's perfect smooth skin she couldn't help the sob of relief that escaped her.

'There are various things that first-born males are more susceptible to than females, but I don't think we missed much when we checked these two over,' Marc said thoughtfully, moving close enough to be heard over the baby's cries. 'They've been kept in the same nursery with their bassinets side by side when they aren't sharing one to come in here with you. You've been feeding them yourself up till now, so it can't be—'

'No, Marc!' Laurel exclaimed as the answer came to her in a blinding flash. At least, she hoped it was the answer. 'They *haven't* been treated the same. Last night Nikolai was hungry and one of the midwives gave him some formula so she didn't have to wake me. Ana didn't have any, but I just gave Nikolai some more in case he wasn't getting enough from me.'

'You think it could be allergy to bottle milk?' Dmitri asked.

'I think it could be,' Laurel agreed. 'I was severely allergic to cow's milk until I was about five.'

'So was I!' Lauren exclaimed. 'I still have to be careful how much cheese I eat.'

Laurel didn't know whether to laugh with relief that they seemed to have come up with the answer or cry at the dilemma that now faced her.

Ana had started crying for her food too, and she barely had enough milk left for one hungry baby, let alone two.

Just when she thought she was going to burst into tears Dmitri sat down beside her on the bed and put an arm around her shoulders. She didn't know how he'd read her mind and he didn't even have to say anything for her to sense his protective strength.

She knew it was weak of her to want him to take over the decision-making, but suddenly her brain just couldn't cope any more. After the trauma of the last half-hour she just wanted someone to wave a magic wand and make everything right.

She should have known that Dmitri would do better than that.

'Bring Ana to me, please,' he directed Lauren. 'Then if you could see if they have any soya-based formula in the nursery. If not, a bottle of glucose water until Laurel has more milk. And we will need clean bedding for Laurel and a nightdress.'

Lauren threw a pointed look at her, the gleam in her eyes reminding Laurel of the special gift her sister had given her. 'Laurel's got a clean nightdress in the cupboard beside her bed,' she pointed out, then hurried out to do Dmitri's bidding.

'Do you want to change your clothing while you wash your hands? I could hold Nikolai, too,' he offered when they were finally on their own for a moment.

'With both of them crying, you'll end up deaf,' she warned, suddenly wondering if she dared to put on that beautiful nightdress. It would certainly pick her spirits up better than her usual tents.

The fact that it would be a reminder to Dmitri of what he was walking away from was an ignoble reason for donning it, but it gave her the bravado to do it.

When she paused in front of the basin to try to see what she looked like, she nearly changed her mind.

'Wow!' she breathed when she caught sight of the lush curves displayed over the sumptuous lace. 'I look a lot better than I feel.'

In fact, the more she looked at the way the silky fabric skimmed her far-from-toned body the better she felt about her appearance, and she realised that the gift had probably done far more than Lauren could have hoped for her morale.

The sound of two babies exercising their lungs at

full stretch reminded her that she'd left Dmitri jug-
gling both of them at once. She took a deep breath
and was still grinning about the way it enhanced her
already impressive assets when she walked back into
the room.

'*Kraseevi!*' Dmitri whispered when he caught sight of
Laurel, completely forgetting they had an audience as
his eyes followed her hungrily.

'Laurel, I hope you don't mind that I started without you,' Lauren said brightly, Nikolai finally silenced by the bottle plugged firmly in his mouth.

Dmitri hoped she hadn't watched him devouring
her sister with his eyes. He felt the heat of a blush
creep into his face and brought his unhappy daughter
up to his cheek in an attempt to hide the fact.

'Here is Mama,' he murmured, suddenly realising
that she looked less like a new mother than a sexy,
exciting woman. And he was supposed to be able to
walk away from her in a matter of hours?

He'd known it was going to be difficult to go—
that's why he'd brought his departure date forward
once he'd known they were all going to be safe. He
just hadn't realised that he was going to be leaving
his heart and soul behind when he went.

All he could do now was to make sure he still had
his pride. It was going to be hard but it wouldn't be
fair to leave Laurel with regrets about a situation that
none of them could change.

Almost as soon as Laurel had silenced Ana with
her delayed meal, Lauren deposited Nikolai in his
arms.

'He needs winding before he has the rest of the

bottle,' she directed briskly, strangely impatient to leave the nephew she'd been so eager to get her hands on.

She fluttered her fingers at Laurel and left, closing the door firmly behind her.

And because Dmitri couldn't think of a single thing to say, the room was filled with the strangely intimate sound of little mouths gulping rhythmically.

For a moment he thought of starting a conversation just for the sake of filling the silence between them, but with so little time left, he didn't want to waste any of it on banalities.

What he wanted to say was that he loved her and that leaving her was going to kill him.

He wanted to tell her that if he had any option, he would be staying in England. To let her know that the thought of not seeing their babies grow and thrive was almost as painful as the thought that he might never see the light making a halo of her hair and turning her into a Christmas angel.

'So, when do you go?' she asked when Ana had finally fallen asleep against her shoulder, sounding so unconcerned that the first cracks began to appear in his heart. Did she truly care so little?

'I go to the *aeraport* tomorrow afternoon, but I take my car to garage in the morning.'

'Your car?' Her mouth lifted in a smile. 'What's wrong with the car you've dreamed of since you were a teenager?'

'Nothing.' He shrugged. What did a car matter if he couldn't have Laurel and their babies? 'They have someone who wants to buy it from me.'

For a moment she looked stricken. He hadn't realised that she might be attached to the compact little sports model he'd bought almost as soon as he'd had his first pay cheque in England. He'd have offered it to her if he'd thought she'd wanted it…but no. It would be impractical with two babies. They would need safety seats and far too much paraphernalia to make it reasonable.

'So, when will you have to leave Edenthwaite to get there on time?'

Frustration that she only seemed to want a detailed itinerary, rather than talk about all the questions that seethed in the air between them, brought him up short.

If that was the way she wanted it, then he would be better off going as soon as possible…but not before he'd told his babies that he loved them and would be thinking about them every day.

At least he had copies of the photos taken in the nursery to supplement his memories. And if he ever got the courage up to come back to England, perhaps Laurel wouldn't mind if he spent some time with them—if she'd even told them who he was.

'*Ya lyublyu ti, Nikolai,*' he whispered as he kissed his son's head for the last time and laid him in the bassinet.

'*Ya lyublyu ti, Ana,*' he said as he laid his daughter beside her brother, knowing they were both too small to know just how much he did love them, and that he'd love them for ever, even from halfway around the world.

Finally it was time to straighten up and face Laurel, hoping he could put a good face on it even though everything was churning around inside him.

'*Spaseeba*, Laurel,' he said, reaching for her hand and absurdly grateful when she let him hold it. 'Thank you for giving me such beautiful babies.'

'You're welcome, Dmitri,' she whispered, and he almost persuaded himself that it was the threat of tears that made her eyes shine. 'Thank you for giving them to me.'

When she retrieved her hand his own was left briefly hanging in mid-air, still feeling the lingering warmth of hers. He should have taken it back and turned to go away, but instead he reached out to stroke the silky tendrils of hair that framed her beautiful face.

'*Ya lyublyu ti, ahnghel,*' he whispered, his voice beyond use. 'Be happy.' Then he turned and strode swiftly out of the room, knowing that he had just moments of control left before he broke down and cried like a child.

The pain in Laurel's chest was so huge that it felt as if it was crushing her heart.

She was off the bed and halfway across the room before she even realised she was moving, then came to her senses.

Where was she going? Running after Dmitri? To what end?

He'd said his goodbyes and told her to be happy. Apart from the fact that it confirmed the fact that he was going, it didn't sound as if he had any intention of coming back.

'So much for the power of the sexy nightdress,' she whispered sadly as she wandered back to her bed.

Looking for something to do—*anything* to do that

would take her mind off the emptiness she was feeling inside—Laurel opened the drawer in the bedside cabinet.

'Teach yourself Russian in twenty easy lessons,' she read on the cover of the paperback volume inside, and had to stifle a sob. Why on earth she'd carried that around with her for the last year, she'd never know. Probably under the mistaken idea that there was the chance of something permanent between Dmitri and herself.

Still, it would give her something to do, working out what he'd said to each of them when he'd said his goodbyes.

It took a while as she juggled the complexities of approximating the sounds she'd heard with the Cyrillic alphabet and then translating them into English.

'I don't believe it!' she exclaimed when the puzzle suddenly unravelled. She leapt to her feet, her heart pounding in her chest with new vigour. 'Why didn't he tell me, the stupid man?'

She desperately wanted to run after him but that was out of the question. He had probably driven away from Denison Memorial ages ago.

'But there is one way to reach him,' she muttered as she rang the bell, impatiently waiting to find out where the nearest phone was situated. 'Mobile phones have their uses.' And he'd given her the number of his in case she needed him for any reason.

Well, she did need him, for the best of all reasons—because she loved him and wanted to spend the rest of her life with him.

'Even if it means moving to Russia for the rest of my life,' she said firmly.

She suffered a brief pang at the thought of leaving the twin she'd just met, but when she put the possibility of a long-distance relationship with a sister against the loss of the man she loved, there was only one choice.

It seemed to take hours before the phone arrived beside her bed and her hands were shaking as she tapped out the numbers.

It rang and rang and for a moment the thought that she was too late.

'Dmitri? It's Laurel,' she said when he finally answered, straining to hear whether he was still in his hotel room, collecting the last of his belongings, or had already set off for the motorway and was now parked in a lay-by somewhere.

Wouldn't it be ironic if it was the same lay-by where he'd stopped that night and heard her trying to start her car?

'Laurel?' He seemed shocked to hear her voice. 'Is something wrong?'

'Yes. Something's very wrong,' she said in a voice that shook with tension. 'I need you to come back to the hospital, please. I need to tell—'

'I am coming now,' he interrupted with fear in his voice, then cut the connection.

Suddenly she realised that her request must have made him think that there was an emergency—something wrong with the babies again. But it was too late to put his mind at rest now. She would have to apologise when he got here.

'But what am I going to say when he *does* get

here?' she demanded aloud, her emotions see-sawing between dread at the possibility of making a complete fool of herself and elation that she was going to see him again. The four walls didn't offer any suggestions and neither did her sleeping babies.

She stopped pacing up and down and drew in a steadying breath as she considered just what was at stake.

'Only my happiness,' she admitted with wry understatement. And if that was the case, why on earth had she spent the last couple of days tiptoeing around the conversation that *should* have been raised as soon as she'd recovered from the delivery?

Because, for all her stubborn determination in the past—in overcoming her addiction, forging a career and evading Robert Wainwright until she could find her twin—she now realised that those were things where failure would ultimately only involve her day-to-day existence.

It was galling to realise that she was a coward when it came to exposing her heart.

She'd known Dmitri for months—worked with him, fallen in love with him, *made* love with him—but had only told him once that she loved him. Even then she'd taken the coward's way out and had written the words on the back of an old envelope.

This time she was going to have to find the courage to do it face to face, and deal with the consequences. This time, if he went away, he would be doing it knowing that she loved him and had been willing to go to Russia with him...

Suddenly, before she was nearly ready for it, she heard Dmitri's familiar stride bringing him towards her door. She whirled to face it, feeling almost like an animal at bay as she gripped the window sill behind her.

'Laurel? What is wrong?' he demanded as he hurried across the room towards her. 'Are the babies…?'

A quick glance told him that they were both asleep, obviously perfectly content now that they had full stomachs.

'Dmitri, I'm sorry I called you like that—made you come all the way back to the hospital,' she apologised, so eager to get the words out that they almost emerged as a gabble.

'It was no problem,' he said soothingly. 'I was already on my way here…'

'I needed to see you to tell you that I've been a coward,' she continued, barely registering what he was saying in her rush to tell him everything. 'It wasn't until I looked the words up in my Russian phrase book that I realised what you'd said to the babies…and to me, and I knew that I should…'

She stopped as his words registered.

'You were already on your way here?' That explained why he'd arrived so quickly. 'Why? Did you forget something?'

'Yes, I forgot something. I forgot to tell you something.'

He took several measured paces towards her so that she could see all too clearly the way the light shone off the dark hair he'd bequeathed to his children and threw shadows of his thick lashes across the lean angles of his cheekbones.

'Before I left, I was a coward, speaking from my heart only in Russian,' he said huskily, those fascinating silvery eyes almost too bright, even from several paces away. 'I had to come back once more to tell you that I love you, and that I'm going to miss you.'

'Oh, Dmitri, you remembered!' she exclaimed as tears welled up in her eyes. 'Those were the same words I used in my note when I had to leave you nearly nine months ago.'

He blinked, a puzzled look bringing his dark brows together. 'What note?'

'The note I left for you. You remember? I wrote it on the back of an envelope from Russia...' Her words faded away in the face of his incomprehension. 'You never saw it? All this time you thought I'd just disappeared and you never knew...?'

Dmitri used an expression that she certainly wouldn't be searching for in her phrase book, then threw his hands up in the air.

'We are both *gloopi*!' he exclaimed, and she had to chuckle at the sound of the word.

'If that means we're stupid, then I agree,' she said, sobering fast. 'All this time I assumed that you knew that I loved you...that I *love* you,' she corrected quickly. 'But when you never said it to me—'

'Until I was leaving,' he interrupted.

'And then you said it in Russian so I had to look it up in my phrase book,' she pointed out in disgust.

'And if I had only said something...maybe nine months or even a year ago, when you first came into my life like an unexpected Christmas gift...?' he suggested. 'But we can never know what would have happened then. *Now*, though, it is different. Now that you know what *"ya lyublyu ti"* means...?'

The expression in his eyes was a perfect mixture of pleading and hope that she couldn't resist, but she had a leading question of her own.

'Is it something that I will be hearing often? I hope so, especially if we're going to be living in Russia.'

'You would come to Russia with me?' he exclaimed in swift delight that was equally swiftly squashed. 'But it is not possible. What about Lauren? You have only just met her. You will want to get to know her after all this time.'

'Ah, Dmitri,' she murmured, unable to bear the distance still between them and determined that there should be as little as possible in the future.

Her hands were trembling slightly as she slid them tentatively up to his shoulders. For all that she was now a mother of two, her practical experience of seduction was still non-existent.

Perhaps her instincts were right because his hands quickly circled her to lock at the back of her waist in an unmistakably possessive way.

She paused a second to savour the feeling, but he was waiting for an answer.

'Dmitri, even though I often longed for a sister, I have lived for twenty-eight years without Lauren. I'm looking forward to catching up on all those years apart but I'm quite prepared to get to know her slowly by letter, by phone, by e-mail…whatever.'

She curved her hands up behind his head, running her fingers through the silky thickness of his hair as she held his gaze and added softly, fervently, 'I have tried to live without you for nearly nine months and I've never been so unhappy. I want to be with you. I *need* to be with you…if that is what you want, too?'

'Ah, *ahnghel*,' he breathed against her mouth before he swung her up into his arms then sat on the side of her bed to cradle her close to his heart. 'Of course I want it, too. You are the gift that I want to keep for ever. More than for ever.'

'You look beautiful,' Lauren said with tears in her eyes as Laurel turned back to face her in the antechamber to the registry office. 'And this is perfect for a Christmas bride.'

Laurel touched a finger to the golden pendant her twin had just fixed around her throat.

Dmitri had given her the perfect little angel to remind her of his private name for her. Because it was so special to the two of them—more of a pledge than a simple gift—she'd wanted to wear it for the ceremony today, but her fingers had been trembling too much to fasten the catch. At the last minute she'd grabbed Lauren and enlisted her help.

'Well, he's waiting inside with Marc and the babies—waiting rather impatiently, too. Are you ready?'

The thought of Dmitri waiting impatiently for her was enough to make her wonder why she was still out here with Lauren.

'I hope you don't mind that we're going to Russia so soon?' she asked, suddenly uncertain that Lauren would understand why she wasn't willing to wait. Apart from Dmitri's honourable insistence on fulfilling his contract with his hospital, there was the love binding him to his Babushka Ana.

'Of course I don't mind...well, I mind, but I also understand,' she said, giving Laurel a hug. 'If it were

Marc, I'd be off like a shot. Anyway, it gives us somewhere different to go for a holiday. Be prepared for frequent visitors!'

And with Laurel's last concern gone, it was time to join Dmitri and their precious babies.

'Till death us do part,' she repeated steadily, looking up into his eyes and knowing that with this man she had been given everything she had ever wanted.

'My Christmas gift,' Dmitri added quietly as he bent to kiss her for the first time as his wife.

'More than a gift, remember?' she murmured as she looked up into silvery eyes full of love. 'Your Christmas angel will be with you for ever.'

Modern Romance™
...seduction and
passion guaranteed

Tender Romance™
...love affairs that
last a lifetime

Sensual Romance™
...sassy, sexy and
seductive

Blaze™
...sultry days and
steamy nights

Medical Romance™
...medical drama on
the pulse

Historical Romance™
...rich, vivid and
passionate

27 new titles every month.

*With all kinds of Romance for
every kind of mood...*

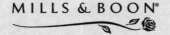

MILLS & BOON®

MILLS & BOON

CHRISTMAS SECRETS

Three Festive Romances

CAROLE MORTIMER   CATHERINE SPENCER
DIANA HAMILTON

Available from 15th November 2002

*Available at most branches of WH Smith,
Tesco, Martins, Borders, Eason, Sainsbury's
and all good paperback bookshops.*

1202/59/MB50

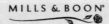

FREE

2 BOOKS
AND A SURPRISE GIFT!

We would like to take this opportunity to thank you for reading this Mills & Boon® book by offering you the chance to take TWO more specially selected titles from the Medical Romance™ series absolutely FREE! We're also making this offer to introduce you to the benefits of the Reader Service™—

★ FREE home delivery   ★ FREE gifts and competitions
★ FREE monthly Newsletter   ★ Exclusive Reader Service discount
★ Books available before they're in the shops

Accepting these FREE books and gift places you under no obligation to buy; you may cancel at any time, even after receiving your free shipment. Simply complete your details below and return the entire page to the address below. **You don't even need a stamp!**

YES! Please send me 2 free Medical Romance books and a surprise gift. I understand that unless you hear from me, I will receive 4 superb new titles every month for just £2.55 each, postage and packing free. I am under no obligation to purchase any books and may cancel my subscription at any time. The free books and gift will be mine to keep in any case.

M2ZEC

Ms/Mrs/Miss/Mr ....Initials ....
BLOCK CAPITALS PLEASE

Surname ....

Address ....

....

....Postcode ....

Send this whole page to:
UK: FREEPOST CN81, Croydon, CR9 3WZ
EIRE: PO Box 4546, Kilcock, County Kildare (stamp required)